FROM: *retroFIB@go2outer.net*
SUBJECT: Interesting Times

A message to our Earth Friends:

These are strange and interesting times!
    We need agents who are prepared to go on a dangerous mission. Only the bravest will succeed.
Here are your instructions:

1. Start reading this book. Your initial password is the first name of the leader of the Hard Fists (in Chapter One).

2. Log on to the Outernet by typing *www.go2outer.net* into your Internet browser, then enter this password to begin your adventure.
    When you have done this, enter your agent ID if you are already a Friend, or register as a new Friend with the FIB. Then check your o-mails — you will receive a message from The Weaver telling you what to do next. Remember to open all your other o-mails and explore your FIB Files and Links. They could contain important, necessary information.
    It is time to stand up and be counted!

Commander Retro
Sector Commander, Epsilon Sector
FIB (Friends Intelligence Bureau)

**Introducing something truly
out of this world . . .**

WWW.GO2OUTER.NET

time out

Steve Barlow and Steve Skidmore

AN
APPLE
PAPERBACK

SCHOLASTIC INC.
New York Toronto London Auckland Sydney
Mexico City New Delhi Hong Kong Buenos Aires

ISBN 0-439-34354-2

12 11 10 9 8 7 6 5 4 3 2 1   3 4 5 6 7 8/0

Printed in the U.S.A.   40
First Scholastic printing, January 2003

FIB ORIENTATION FILE:
FRIENDS INTELLIGENCE BUREAU

THIS IS A TOP-SECURITY-PROTECTED FILE FOR FRIENDS EYES ONLY. THIS INFORMATION MUST NOT BE COPIED, DUPLICATED, OR REVEALED TO ANY BEING NOT VERIFIED AS A FRIEND OF THE OUTERNET.

)(**Info Byte 1 — The Outernet:** The pan-galactic web of information. Created by The Weaver for the free exchange of information between all advanced beings in the Galaxy.

)(**Info Byte 2 — The Server:** Alien communication device and teleportation portal. The last such device is in the hands of the Friends of the Outernet.

)(**Info Byte 3 — Friends:** Forces who are loyal to The Weaver in the struggle to free the Outernet from the clutches of The Tyrant.

)(**Info Byte 4 — FOEs:** The Forces of Evil, creatures loyal to The Tyrant, who seek to use the Outernet to control and oppress the people of the Galaxy.

⋇ **Info Byte 5 — Bitz and Googie:** Shape-shifting aliens disguised as a dog and a cat, respectively. Bitz is a Friends agent (code-named Sirius) and ally of Janus. Googie (code-named Vega) was formerly a FOEs agent but claims now to be loyal to the Friends.

⋇ **Info Byte 6 — Janus:** A Friends Agent who, while trying to keep The Server from the FOEs, disappeared into N-space.

⋇ **Info Byte 7 — Jack Armstrong:** A fourteen-year-old human from England who became responsible for the fate of The Server when it was given to him as a birthday present. **Merle Stone** and **Lothar (Loaf) Gelt:** Jack's American friends from the nearby U.S. Air Force Base who have been helping him keep The Server safe from the FOEs.

PROLOGUE

Selenity Dreeb stared sadly at his computer screen.

There was a single line of text on the screen. The message was:

Hi, Koffkoff!

(Actually, it was nothing of the kind, because the written Veredian language is one of complex wedge shapes arranged in a confusing variety of combinations. This version is subtitled.)

Selenity had sent the message three minutes ago. It would take another eight minutes and twenty seconds for Koffkoff's reply to reach Selenity's computer. And when it did, it would probably say something dumb like, "Hi, Selenity!"

Selenity caught the eye of his pet spider-monkey, Tig, who was sitting on top of the screen waiting for it to do something interesting. The monkey waved its eight legs and chittered.

Time, thought Selenity. *That was the problem.* He clicked his beak in annoyance and with one of his four hands reached for the science magazine that lay half open beside his computer keyboard. He read:

A Short History of Time
by Seething Hawkthing

In many parts of the known Galaxy, life-forms have developed strange and exotic ways of measuring time. In countless worlds, our ancestors from long ago cut out gigantic stones from rock and hauled them over long distances in order to create huge temples to measure time by the movements of the stars.

Selenity nodded to himself. There were some temples like that on Vered II. But now nobody could remember how they were supposed to work. What was left of them were just piles of rocks that Veredians used for picnics, if the weather was nice. Or they could be used for a game of Veredian-Rules Soccer, only there were too many goals and they were too narrow.

A message appeared on the screen underneath Selenity's greeting. Sure enough, it said,

Hi, Selenity!

Selenity groaned and tapped at the keyboard. A third line of text appeared on the screen:

How are things chillin' where you are?

Selenity sent the message, annoyed with the realization that it would take at least another eleven minutes and twenty seconds for Koffkoff's reply to arrive, and turned his attention back to the magazine article.

Some life-forms have wanted to measure time in order to predict tides or seasons, times for planting or harvest. Other beings have simply wanted to be able to point out to other beings (with smug little smiles) *exactly* how late they are.

Time has been measured in a confusing variety of ways — some of which have been spectacularly unsuccessful, like the Pointless Sundials of the planet Dark, or the Dessicated Waterclock of WattaScorcha, the desert planet.

Most life-forms treat time like some sort of giant cake, dividing it into smaller and smaller slices. On the planet Zhilqueeg, for example, there are eighty neehees in a gajug, fifty gajugs in a twip, twenty-two twips in a yuryur, and so on, bringing about the common expression on Zhilqueeg: "There just aren't enough twips in the yuryur."

But on Vered II, time is treated rather differently. The Veredians know that time exists. They know that time passes for everybody at the same rate. They just don't see why they should all have to agree, at any particular moment in their lives, what time it "is."

There are clocks on Vered II because the Veredians find the ticking restful. But they

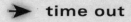

don't see why every instant of their lives has to be counted and ordered by some soulless machine. So, around the faces of the Great Clock of Vered II, there are no numbers.

There are question marks.

This means, of course, that the time on Veredian clocks is always the time they want it to be — breakfast time, breaktime, bedtime, depending whether they are hungry, tired, or sleepy when they glance at their numberless clocks and say, "Goodness, is that the time?" And when a Veredian says, "There's no time like the present," it's very difficult to argue.

Selenity put the magazine down. *That was all fine,* he thought unhappily. *But there was a problem. Although we Veredians may choose to ignore time, time doesn't choose to ignore us.*

Selenity could chat and play games with his other friends on the Vered Wide Web pretty much in real time. None of their machines was more than a few thousand miles away from one another, so the time-delay from their computers to his was a few seconds at the most.

But the environmental dome protecting the small colony on Vered III, where Koffkoff now lived, was sixty-two-and-a-half million miles away from Selenity's bedroom. At the speed of light, 186,000 miles per second, it took five minutes and forty seconds for Selenity's messages to reach Koffkoff, and the same amount of time for Koffkoff's replies to reach Selenity. So their conversations tended to be pretty slow. And the amount of time Selenity spent on the Net caused his mother and all three of his fathers (Veredian parenting arrangements are pretty complicated) to moan constantly about phone bills. Sometimes Selenity wondered why he bothered keeping in touch with Koffkoff. Then he remembered it was because Koffkoff was the only real friend he had. Selenity didn't get out much.

"Selenity!"

"Yes, Mom?"

His mother's voice floated up from the floor below. "Have you taken the vidi-books back to the shop yet?"

Selenity groaned. "No, Mom. I'll do it later.

I'm chatting with Koffkoff." There was an exasperated sigh from the hole where the climbing pole led to the living area of the Dreebs'
tree house. Selenity turned back to the screen
and tapped the fingers of his four hands as he
waited for Koffkoff's reply.

Selenity's computer looked as if it had been
thrown together from a variety of components
that had been designed for other purposes. It
had. Selenity's computer was one great big
kludge-up. Not that he cared. Most of his con-
tacts on the Vered Net probably had machines
that looked as crazy as his, even crazier. There
was no point waiting for the big electronics
manufacturers to get their act together. That
wasn't how Selenity and his group stayed
ahead of the game.

Another message was coming in from Koffkoff. The new line read:

I'm fine, how are you?

Selenity slumped back in his seat. Tig
looked at his master with his head on one side
and gave a worried chirp. Selenity beckoned,
and the spider-monkey glided over on its hairy
legs and climbed onto Selenity's top left shoul-

9

der. Selenity rubbed Tig's fur with one pair of hands. With the other pair, he wrote:

> *Look, Koffkoff, we have to make these messages more interesting or it'll take forever just to say hello!*

Selenity thought for a minute, then went on.

Wouldn't it be great if we could send and receive signals to each other instantly? I know we can't, until somebody invents some sort of signal that goes faster than the speed of light — some sort of hyperspace communication, like they have in the teevee shows. But I guess that's impossible. It takes three years to get reports from the frontier post in the Tarantibi system, and that's just the next star over!

Do you think computers on different worlds will ever be able to communicate instantly across interplanetary — even interstellar — distances, so that everyone in the Galaxy can share knowledge?

Selenity's mother stuck her head up through the hole in the floor. Her ears were

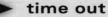

flattened and her four nostrils flared with annoyance. "Selenity!"

"I told you, Mom! I'll take the books back later!"

"Not later, Selenity. Not soon. Do it now, or I'll turn off your computer!"

"Yes, Mom." Selenity's crest drooped in resignation. With a sigh, he pressed the key to send his message and plodded across to the climbing pole where his mother dumped the vidi-books into his arms.

His mother pointed to the gathering gloom outside. "Scoot!"

As the carrier-wave carrying Selenity's message sped into space, pausing for a barely measurable fraction of a second in the circuits of a communications satellite to collect itself for a leap across the vast distances between worlds, it passed an incoming signal. A signal whose origin Selenity would have found very surprising. A signal that was about to change his life — and the life of every intelligent being in the Galaxy — forever. . . .

CHAPTER ONE

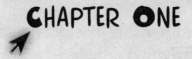

**Vered II, Eridanus System
100 Gala-years ago**

A series of blinding blue-white flashes shot through the dripping forest canopy. As these faded, five figures formed from the after-image and looked around carefully.

"Teleportation is the worst," complained Loaf. He stretched and stared at the lush vegetation that surrounded the traveling companions. Huge trees reached into the darkness above and hundreds of tree creepers and vines dangled down from the giant branches that stretched out across the darkening sky.

"Looks like we're in the middle of a forest," said Jack.

"Good eye, man-cub." Loaf applauded sarcastically. "But what are we doing here?"

Jack nodded toward the black laptop computer in his hands. "Getting The Server to The Weaver like Janus said."

"Yeah, yeah, we know," said Loaf sourly, "so The Weaver and the Friends can defeat The Tyrant and the FOEs, and blah, blah, blah." He glared angrily at The Server. "That thing keeps teleporting us into every trouble-spot around the Galaxy looking for The Weaver, and we don't know who or what The Weaver is, or even whether it really exists at all. I'm starting to think there ain't no such thing. Yuck!"

Somewhere above, a leaf had tipped and sent a stream of chilly water cascading down the back of Loaf's neck. He wriggled inside his suddenly damp New York Giants shirt. "And this place doesn't look any better than the other low-rent neighborhoods we've ended up in." He looked around nervously. "Too many trees, too many shadows. There could be anything in there."

"Such as?" purred the cat winding itself around Merle's legs.

Loaf glared down at Googie. "Such as giant *ann-ie-con-das* that wrap themselves around their prey — like cats, for instance — and squeeze them until their brains come out their ears like toothpaste from a tube."

Googie gave him a scornful glance. "Anacondas live in South America, and this is not Earth." Nevertheless, she stayed close to Merle.

Merle shook her head. "I don't think this *is* a forest, as we know it. It looks like some giant botanical garden. Look at those." She pointed toward a series of walkways suspended high above the forest floor. Beyond these, nestled among the trees, were several clear domes that glowed with internal lights.

Jack looked down at the small dog at his feet. "Any ideas, Bitz?"

Bitz gave a doggy grin. "We must be in dog heaven. Look at all those trees!" His rear leg twitched and a thread of saliva dribbled from his mouth.

"You are so *basic,*" spat Googie, licking her paw. "Never mind where we are, have the FOEs got a trace on us?"

Jack shrugged. "I don't know, but The Server can tell us. Help!"

Ching!

A silver holographic head shot out of The Server and shimmered over the keyboard. "Kludge! That trip has phase-changed my circuits!"

"What's the problem?" asked Loaf.

"There's no problem, monkey-brain," snapped Help. "It just so happens that I've never done time travel before, and I've got some polymorphic kludges messing up my innards."

Jack stared at the hologram. "So we've actually traveled back in time?"

"You'd better believe it," replied Help. "We've just undergone a time-teleportation experience through the courtesy of t-t-mail. And that wasn't a stutter."

"So where are we?"

"*When* are we?"

"Hey, one at a time! We *were* on planet Helios, we're *now* on Vered II, a forest planet in the Eridanus System. Lucky for you primates, there's plenty of trees for you to climb and leaves to wipe your . . ."

"Wait a cotton-pickin' minute!" Bitz was staring at the hologram. "Vered II? You have to be kidding me! This can't be Vered II — that's where Janus and I found The Server before we came to Earth. It didn't look anything like this!"

Help frowned ferociously. Hologramatic steam poured from his ears. "Listen, dog-breath, are you calling me a liar?!"

"Lighten up," interrupted Merle. "Maybe you're both right. How far back in time have we come?"

Help gave Bitz another filthy look as it calculated. "At a rough estimate, about a hundred Gala-years."

Merle shrugged. "There you go. A place can change a lot in a hundred years."

"Not this much," muttered Bitz, looking unhappy and unconvinced.

"Have the FOEs got a trace on us?" demanded Googie. "Do they know we're here?"

"Give me time," muttered Help. The hologram's eyes spun around for a second or two. "No. There's nothing. I can't locate any kind of Outernet signal from Friends or FOEs."

"How can that be?" asked Merle.

"We've gone back," replied Help, "to a time before the Outernet existed. The first gateway for what became the Galaxy Wide

Web was set up here in the Eridanus Sector just about a hundred years before I had the pleasure (ha!) of meeting you monkeys. Now, leave me alone. I've got some readjusting to do." The hologram disappeared back into The Server.

Merle looked thoughtful. "Then the time we've come back to is the time when the Outernet was first created. Maybe we have to do something to help get it started. That could be why Janus fixed The Server, so we could go back in time."

Loaf scowled. "Maybe — could be — we don't *know* anything!"

"Then we'd better start finding out." Jack nodded toward the mass of greenery. "Let's see what's in there."

Bitz eyed the trees. He perked up and wagged his tail. "Nice call!"

Selenity looked at the titles of his vidi-books and sighed. *Star Trees, Close Encounters of the Tree Kind, Lost in Spruce, The Maytreex,* and *E.T. The Extratreestrial.* They were his favorite sci-story titles, and he'd been so busy with his computer that he hadn't had time to scan any of them more than three or four times.

Selenity slid down the climbing pole to the walkway below his family's tree house. He reached up with two of his arms, grabbed hold of the vines hanging from the trees — vine swinging was more fun than the walkways of Vered City, and a lot faster — and set off to the vidi-library. Tig raced alongside him, the spider-monkey's eight legs giving it a distinct swinging advantage, especially as Selenity had the vidi-books clasped in his lower set of arms. Every now and then, Tig scrambled up a tree trunk to nibble on a leaf before swinging after Selenity.

They soon reached Green Square. Selenity dropped down onto a walkway and made his way across the central meeting place of Vered City. Green Square was built on a huge platform made from organic plastic, several hundred feet above the forest floor. Yellow-blue flares lit up the shops and cafés that surrounded the square and the dozens of walkways that led to and from the surrounding forest.

Towering over the square was the Numberless Clock of Vered II. Veredian engineers had constructed the clock in the tallest tree on the planet. Four giant clock dials were set around the trunk, so that all could see what time it wasn't as the hands swept around the question marks on the huge white clock faces.

Around the trunk of the clock was a number of wooden statues of famous Veredian characters: the explorer Leaf Ericson; Holly Wood, the teevee star; and Forest Grump, the all-Veredian hero. Jets of water cascaded from several fountains and a stream flowed across the square before crashing downward to the forest floor. Spray from the gushing waterfall misted across the square.

Selenity crossed the square, barely noticing other Veredians going about their daily business at their own pace. Some stood around, passing the time with friends, others sat and perched on café benches, reading newspapers, drinking tree juice from huge green leaves, or pecking at plates of nuts and seeds. Selenity had no time for this; he glanced up at the Great Clock. *It should be Playing-on-My-Computer Time,* he thought, and decided to take a shortcut to the vidi-library. It was a choice that would change the future of the Galaxy.

Selenity jumped over the side of the walkway, grabbed hold of a tree vine and began to spin down it. Tig gave a playful squeak and followed. The two of them spun wildly down the stringy creeper, deeper into the darkness beneath the lighted walkways of the city. Selenity felt himself getting dizzy. He let go of the vine, dropped onto a shadowy lower walkway, and realized he'd made a big mistake.

Standing a few yards in front of him was a gang of ten Veredian kids. They wore black shirts and black combat shorts. Selenity recognized them immediately: the Hard Fists.

Selenity thought about scampering back up the vine. But he was too late.

"Well, look who just dropped in. Dreeb the Weeb."

Selenity winced. Tyro Rhomer had spotted him.

Tyro was Selenity's classmate at Vered City High School. However, that's where any similarity between the two ended. Selenity was younger and way more intelligent than Tyro. It

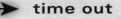

took all of Tyro's brainpower to remember not to drag all four knuckles on the ground.

Selenity kept to himself, preferring to spend time on his computer or scanning vidi-books, while Tyro was the self-appointed leader of the Hard Fists. They spent their time looking for trouble — a pursuit in which they got straight A's.

Tyro approached Selenity with a smile and a swagger. Two of his hands held metal clubs. The other two were clenched. The rest of the gang followed close behind.

Tig's hair stood on end. He leaped onto Se-lenity's shoulder and chirped nervously. Despite his own fear, Selenity gave the monkey a reassuring pat as Tyro stood over him, eyeing him with contempt.

"What brings you out of your tree house, Dreeb? I thought you'd be staring at your computer, contacting your fellow weebs." Tyro burst into mocking laughter. The Hard Fists followed their leader, beaks chattering as they guffawed.

Suddenly, Tyro reached over, snatched Tig, and held him up by the tail. The monkey screeched with fright and struggled, trying vainly to get free.

Despite the knot of fear in his stomach, Selenity was angered enough to cry out, "Put the monkey down."

Tyro held Tig in front of Selenity's beak. "Make me," he taunted.

Selenity backed down. Tyro laughed and flung Tig to the ground. The spider-monkey picked itself up, chittering unhappily, and crawled painfully to hide behind Selenity's legs.

Tyro glanced down at the vidi-books in Selenity's hands. "Books!" he mocked. "Reading?! Hur-hur-hur!" He turned to his followers. "Do we need books? I don't think so." He faced Selenity again. "What's the point of reading, eh?"

Selenity's four nostrils flared. Before he could stop himself, he heard himself say, "You should try it sometime, Tyro. Then maybe you wouldn't be so stupid."

There was a shocked silence. The Hard Fists looked expectantly at Tyro. The air around Selenity suddenly seemed very cold. Tyro's eyes narrowed. The black-shirted bully

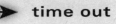

moved threateningly toward Selenity, gently tapping the two metal clubs against each other.

Selenity gulped. *Me and my big beak!* he thought. *Which part of my body is going to get hit first?*

Tyro held one of the clubs under Selenity's chin. "Guess what time it is," he said with quiet menace.

Selenity shrugged.

"It's Teaching-You-a-Lesson Time."

This was different from Selenity's view. He decided it was Get-out-of-Here-Now Time. He turned and ran.

Jack and his companions had been walking for some time. With difficulty, they had made their way from the forest floor onto the suspended walkways. They were all tired, hungry, and grouchy.

Loaf swatted at the irritating flylike insects that constantly buzzed around their heads. "What is the point of walking around this alien garden center waiting to bump into whoever we're supposed to bump into?" he moaned. "It's not going to happen!"

He was wrong.

The travelers rounded a corner and stopped quickly. On the walkway ahead, a pack of black-shirted, four-armed, two-legged creatures was chasing after another four-armed being.

"Hey, we *are* on Vered!" exclaimed Bitz. "Those four-armed guys are Veredians. There's even a spider-monkey."

The fleeing Veredian stumbled and was immediately surrounded by the black-shirted figures. A cry of fear rang through the trees.

"He's in trouble!" cried Jack.

"He sure is," growled Bitz. "The guys in black look like the Hard Fists. I've had trouble with them before."

"Tell us about it later," said Jack. "Come on! We've got to save him!"

"How do you know it's a him?" asked Loaf. "Anyway, why should we get involved?"

"Because there's one of him and about ten of them," snapped Jack.

Loaf shrugged. "That sounds to me like a good reason for helping *them*."

The victim's cries grew louder.

"I don't believe you, Loaf!" said Merle dis-

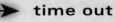

gustedly. "If you ever thought about anybody else, you'd find that people would like you a lot more. Especially if you showed some guts."

Loaf nodded at the group of thugs. "I like my guts where they are: inside my skin."

Merle snorted in annoyance. "You're pathetic."

"We don't have time for this. Come on!" Jack began to race toward the black-shirted creatures, shouting and waving his arms. The others followed.

Tyro and the Hard Fists looked up from giving their "lesson." Ten beaks dropped open with disbelief. Three strange and terrifying two-legged, two-armed creatures and two smaller, four-legged beings were hurtling toward them. These were numbers of limbs that didn't add up for the Hard Fists.

"Only two arms!" screamed one of the gang.

"No beaks!" cried another.

"Droopy skin!"

"Mini-monsters!" One of the gang pointed to Bitz and Googie.

"Aliens!"

The Hard Fists forgot about their "fun," threw their arms in the air, and fled, flinging themselves off the walkway and scampering up (and down) vines. Within seconds, they had disappeared, leaving their victim lying on the walkway.

Selenity looked up in a daze. Tig flung his arms around his master's neck and screeched threats and insults at the incredibly strange creatures who were now standing above them. They were humanoid figures like the ones in Selenity's sci-story vidi-books. One had darker skin than the two others and seemed to be female.

All three humanoids wore loose-fitting clothes and one had some kind of a head-covering that looked like a beak facing backward. Lower to the ground, two four-legged furry creatures stood staring at him. Selenity wondered if Tyro's gang had clobbered him into dreamland.

One of the humanoids held out a strange, five-fingered hand. Hesitantly, Selenity reached up, took it, and was pulled to his feet. "What are you?" he asked with a mixture of fear and relief.

"Friends," replied Jack. "Looks like we turned up just in time."

Selenity's ears perked up in surprise. "I can understand you," he said.

"And we can understand you." Merle pointed at The Server. "This is translating what we all say."

"Are you aliens?" asked Selenity.

Jack laughed. "I suppose so. I'll explain later. But I think we should get out of here, just in case that gang decides to come back. Is there somewhere we can go?"

Selenity nodded. "We could go to my house."

"Is it far? You saw how the others reacted to us. We don't want to start a panic."

Selenity nodded. "We can sneak around back."

Jack grinned. "Lead the way."

The trip back to Selenity's tree house was uneventful. The young Veredian was surprisingly calm about the fact that he had just been rescued by extra-tree-estrials; and Jack, Loaf, and Merle had encountered so many alien life-forms in the past few days that they were becoming bored with meeting new species.

Soon the group was standing beside Selenity's climbing-pole.

The Veredian pointed. "Up here." Tig raced up the pole, followed by Selenity. Googie followed. Bitz stood on the walkway looking up. "You're going to have to carry me."

Loaf looked at the pole and then at Bitz. "No way."

Merle stared at Loaf. "I suppose you'll have enough trouble getting *yourself* up there."

"Oh, yeah?" Loaf clenched his fists and thumped them against his chest. "Aaah-ah-ah-ah-ah, ahahahaaaaah! Me Tarzan. You Jane."

Merle rolled her eyes. "You idiot. Me not impressed."

"Well, watch this!" Loaf leaped up, clutched at the climbing pole, and skidded down slowly, ending up lying facedown on the walkway.

Merle used his back as a step. "See you up there."

*   *   *

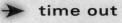

Eventually, after a long struggle, the travelers regrouped in Selenity's study-sleeping room.

"I've got to tell Koffkoff about this!" Selenity headed for his computer.

"Selenity!" The voice came from the lower part of the house.

Everyone froze. "Yes, Mom?" answered Selenity.

"Did you get rid of the vidi-books?"

Selenity groaned. He'd dropped them in his escape from Tyro. That would cost him. "Yes, Mom," he said truthfully.

"What's all the noise? Have you got someone up in your room?"

"Tell her we're your friends," whispered Jack.

Selenity shook his head. "That's a dead giveaway. I haven't got any friends."

"Selenity?"

"They're just some people I met . . . at the vidi-library."

"Do I know them?"

Selenity looked at the group standing before him. "I don't think so, Mom."

"Well, play quietly and don't make a mess. I'm going shopping."

There was the sound of a door closing. "She's gone." Selenity breathed a sigh of relief.

"Be quiet. Don't make a mess," mimicked Loaf. "That's moms for you — a king-size pain in the butt all over the Galaxy. They should be banned."

"Why don't you shut up, Loaf?" snapped Merle. "What do you know?"

There was an uneasy silence. Jack silently cursed Loaf. Merle's mother had died in a crash years ago. Merle had only her father. And as the commander of a fighter wing of the U.S. Air Force, Colonel Stone had little time for his daughter.

Trying to change the subject, Jack pointed at the assortment of green plastic cylindrical boxes and vidi-screens that sat on various benches and tables. A jungle of wires stretched out across the room. "So what's this, Selenity?" he asked.

"My computer," replied Selenity proudly.

"Man, that is so low-tech," sneered Loaf. "That stuff went out with the Ark."

Jack shook his head. "Are you going for

the world record for upsetting as many species as you can? Remember, Loaf, we didn't have this kind of stuff on Earth a hundred years ago."

Loaf shrugged. "I call it like I see it."

Selenity patted one of the boxes. "It's only the beginning. We're building up our system, developing it."

"We? I thought you said you didn't have any friends," Loaf pointed out.

Selenity shrugged. "Not friends exactly, we're more like a group of computer enthusiasts. We've set up our own user group." Selenity smiled proudly. "The Western Eridanus Association of Virtual Electronics and Robotics Systems."

"Snappy title," said Loaf. Jack shot him a look.

Thankfully, Selenity didn't pick up on Loaf's sarcasm. "That's the long version," he explained. "The acronym is better. W - E - A - V - E - R - S. We call ourselves the WEAVERS."

There was a very long silence.

"Have I said something wrong?" Selenity looked hard at his rescuers.

Merle was the first to reply. "We've been looking for you."

Selenity looked puzzled. "How?"

Merle shook her head. "It doesn't matter how. You're The Weaver. We've found you. We've completed our mission!"

CHAPTER TWO

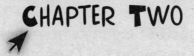

Merle clenched her fists and glared at Jack in frustration. "What are you stalling for? We've done what Janus said we had to do. We've found The Weaver."

"So you've been saying for the last ten minutes." Jack shook his head slowly. "We might have found The Weaver, or this whole thing could just be a weird coincidence. We don't know for sure."

"Oh, come on!" Merle made an impatient gesture. "What do you want?" She pointed a shaky finger at Selenity, who gave a startled squeak and ducked behind a leaf-screen. "You heard what he said. Selenity and his friends are The Weaver. They started the Outernet — or they're going to. That must be why Janus sent us here."

Loaf stared at Selenity's homemade equipment. "You're saying the Outernet got started on this stuff? Get real! I've seen washing machines with more memory! If you tried to download . . ."

"Download!" Merle snapped her fingers. "I'll bet that's what Janus wants us to do. Download information from The Server so that Selenity and his pals — the Weavers — can get a head start creating the Outernet."

"You're just guessing," said Jack patiently. "Selenity's group call themselves the Weavers. Plural. Not The Weaver. We can't hand The Server over to somebody we've only just met on the strength of a guess. We have to be sure."

Merle's eyes flashed dangerously. "What are you trying to pull here, Jack?"

Jack stared at her. "What do you mean?"

"Please?" Jack looked around. Selenity had raised his head cautiously from his hiding place and was waving two of his hands to get their attention. "I don't understand any of this," he said sadly. "Did I say something wrong?"

Jack sighed. "No, it's not your fault. Bitz,

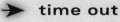

could you fill Selenity in?" Jack led Merle to the far side of the room where they continued their disagreement in fierce whispers.

Loaf was looking around Selenity's bedroom with a snooty expression. "Say, buddy! You got any food around here?"

Selenity blinked both sets of eyelids. "There are probably some nuts and berries in the pantry."

"Nuts and berries?" Loaf responded in disgust. "See, the thing is, you must have me all confused with Yogi Bear. I'm talking about food! Steaks, burgers, doughnuts . . ." Selenity looked puzzled. "Oh, brother!" Loaf's gaze searched hungrily around the room. His eyes fell on a juicy-looking nut, about the size and shape of a mango. Loaf shrugged. It would have to do for now.

Selenity watched in horrified disbelief as Loaf picked up the nut and started to bang it on the table to crack the shell. With a squeal of terror, the small Veredian snatched the fruit just as Loaf was about to try to bite a hole in the shell. Selenity sprang to the other side of the room and cradled the fruit in his hands as carefully as if it were the finest china. Jack and

Merle stopped arguing and stared at Selenity, then to Loaf, and back again.

Loaf glared at his Veredian host. "Hey! I was going to eat that!"

Selenity gave him a strange look. "That wouldn't have been a good idea. This is a Veredian exploding pine nut."

"What is a Veredian exploding pine?" asked Merle.

Selenity gestured carefully. "These trees are. All of them. It's the most common species on Vered. The exploding pine releases its seeds when they hit the ground and its seed cases burst."

Merle nodded. "We have trees that do that back home."

Selenity gave her a teasing look. "I guess maybe our trees are a little more enthusiastic. Watch."

Selenity took the pine nut to the window, held it out carefully over the long drop to the forest floor, and let go.

Nothing happened.

Loaf snorted. "So what's the big deal?"

There was a loud but muffled *whump!*

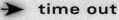

from far below. An orange flash lit up the room. A cloud of leaf debris mushroomed past the window. The tree shook.

Loaf turned pale. "What would have happened if I'd eaten that?"

"You'd have some serious stomach issues that I wouldn't want to be around for," said Merle nastily. She turned to Selenity. "Do those things fall on the city?"

Selenity shook his head. "We harvest the ones in the upper branches. The ones that fall from the lower branches can't do any damage, so we let them explode to get new trees. I'm not supposed to have one in the house." He shrugged. "But they're perfectly safe, as long as you don't drop them."

"Crazy planet," grumbled Loaf. He pulled his baseball cap down over his eyes and lay on a mass of springy branches that had been woven together to make something like a sofa. "Wake me up when there's food available," he ordered the world in general. "The sort that doesn't fight back." He closed his eyes. Jack said something to Merle, and the fight was on again.

Bitz shook his head at the arguing humans and gave a doggy sigh. "Hey, Help! You want to show yourself to our new Friend?"

A crabby-looking hologramatic head popped into view, hovering over The Server's keyboard. "Oh, great! Now the mutt's giving me orders."

Selenity moved closer. His eyes, wide with astonishment, were focused on Help. "Is that a hologram?"

"What's it to you, beaky?" demanded Help.

Selenity examined The Server with an awestruck expression. "Then this thing really is a computer?"

"A computer?" Help's eyes spun in opposite directions before settling on Selenity with a furious glare. Holographic steam poured out of its ears. "Who are you calling a computer? How'd you like it if I called you an amoeba?"

"Ignore him," Bitz told Selenity. "He's been kind of cranky lately."

"I evolved from the primitive calculating machines you call computers," Help persisted in lofty tones, "in much the same way that your species evolved from wriggly things living in primeval swamps. But my evolution

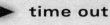

had much more impressive results. Computer! Ha! It's about time a certain application was shown a bit of respect around here."

Selenity regarded Help with respect. "That is so leafy!"

Bitz shot a glance at Help. "Leafy?"

"Veredian for 'cool,'" snapped Help. "I'm trying to translate local speech patterns. Is that all right with you, Mister Scratchy?"

"Simultaneous translation. Twigtastic!" Selenity regarded Help with awe. "What else can you do?"

Help gave him a furious look. "What else *can* I do? I *can* tell you the entire history and future of the universe. I *can* play you the sounds of color. I *can* show you the elemental dance in the heart of a star. I *can* explain chaos theory to nineteen decimal places." Help snorted. "But if you're asking me what I *do* do, I act as a wet nurse and bag carrier for a bunch of no-brain organic life-forms. Talk about a waste! I could cry."

Bitz growled at the hologram. "Do you mind? The only reason I asked you to show your ugly mug was so I could explain about the Outernet to this kid."

Help gave a disdainful sniff. "Oh, don't mind me. Pretend I'm not here, which is what you do most of the time, anyway. I'm sure I can find some horribly dull and meaningless tasks to waste my precious run-time on."

"Why don't you do that?" While Help grumbled to itself, Bitz explained to Selenity, "This device is The Server. It connects us to the Outernet, the pan-Galactic web containing all the knowledge of the Galaxy."

"Wow!" Selenity's eyes threatened to pop out of his head. "Show me!"

"What this dumb mutt should have said," purred Googie, springing onto the tabletop beside The Server, "is that it *would* be able to connect us with the Outernet if the Outernet existed."

"Hey, slinky!" snapped Help. "Get your furry butt outta my face!" Googie growled and swiped at the hologram with her paw, which went straight through it. "Yeah!" Help taunted. "Can't catch me!" Help's head shot around the keyboard as Googie pounced and batted furiously. Bitz rolled his eyes.

Selenity gave Bitz a puzzled look. "But you said The Server could connect you to . . ."

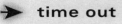

Bitz sighed. "That's where it all gets a bit tricky. See, we're from the future."

Selenity looked blank. "The future?"

"That's right. In the future, the Outernet exists. The Weaver created it to allow all the beings of the Galaxy to share knowledge. But then The Tyrant came along . . ."

"The Tyrant?"

"The Tyrant is the bad guy." Googie had stopped trying to catch Help and was now cleaning herself as if she'd never tried to do anything so silly before. "He wants to use the Outernet to control everything and everybody in the Galaxy. So he sent the FOEs . . ."

"The FOEs?"

Googie gave an angry hiss. "Is there an echo in here? Be quiet and listen. The FOEs are the Forces of Evil. They're trying to take over the Outernet. The Friends are trying to stop them. We're Friends."

"Really?" Selenity cast an uncertain eye over the cat and dog, then glanced at the corner where Jack was glaring at Merle, who was wagging a finger in his face.

"Friends with a capital *F.* Friends of the Outernet. Anyway, this is the only Server not controlled by The Tyrant. If he gets hold of it, the whole Galaxy is a deceased waterfowl."

"A what?"

Bitz glared at Help. The hologram glared back. "Okay, okay. A dead duck. You think simultaneous translation into two languages is easy?"

Selenity was thinking hard. "But if all this is happening in the future . . ."

"Yeah, I'm pretty unclear on that part myself." Bitz scratched his left ear with his hind leg.

Googie looked disgusted. "You've been in that body too long."

Selenity gave her the look of someone who, having lost the plot, believes he's found it again only to discover that he's picked up the wrong book. "Excuse me?"

"The dog and I," explained Googie impatiently, "are chameleoids. Shape-shifters. We got stuck in these shapes. You can't think we evolved into these life-forms on purpose?"

Selenity couldn't think of a reasonable answer to this, so he said, "Er . . ."

"Jumpin' Jack Flash!" snapped Bitz. "Lis-

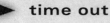

ten, what we figure is, we've been sent way back into the past, which is your present, to take The Server to The Weaver."

"And you think I might be this Weaver?" Selenity stared at Bitz with his beak hanging wide open.

"That's the idea. And if you are, we have to give you The Server. Because if Merle's right, it can tell you guys what you need to know so you can get a head start creating the Outernet."

"Hey!" protested Help, "don't I get a say in this? You think you can just pass me around like a hot potato? This sounds like a bum deal to me." The hologram eyed its surroundings with disgust. "Look at this place! Talk about retro! At least you humans got advanced enough to come down out of the trees."

Selenity was still struggling with a much earlier part of the dialogue. "Me, The Weaver? That's crazy! I'm just a kid who messes around with computers."

"See?" A yell of triumph brought Selenity's head snapping around to the corner where the two humans were arguing. The one called

Jack had evidently heard this last remark and was looking victoriously at the one called Merle. "He says he's not The Weaver."

Merle stamped her foot, sending several dozen leaves spiraling to the floor. "Don't give me that. Maybe he doesn't know he's The Weaver. Maybe he hasn't become The Weaver yet. But that's not what this is about, is it?"

Jack gave her a blank stare. "Isn't it?"

"You can't fool me." Merle's look was scornful. "You just don't want to let go of your little moment of glory."

"What do you mean?"

"The minute you hand The Server over, that's the end of your glorious quest. Isn't it? You stop rocketing around saving the Galaxy like Luke Skywalker and Captain Kirk rolled into one. And you don't want that. Make a landing on Planet Real! You don't want to find The Weaver!"

Jack looked stunned. "That's not true."

"Oh, isn't it?" Merle said, crying angrily. "I want to end this! I want to go home to my dad! I ran out on him — remember? — just when he needed me. He's only got me since my mom died." She turned to Loaf. "Which you so tactfully reminded me about, thank you very much."

Loaf cracked open an eyelid. "Hey, leave me out of this."

"But you don't care about that, do you?" Merle turned her attention back to Jack. "You want to keep fooling around, making like the big hero, just so you don't have to go back to being the two-bit nobody you were before all this started!"

"Whoa!" Loaf looked up and grinned unpleasantly at Jack. "She sure told you, amigo."

Jack felt as if he'd just stepped under a cold shower. "Is that what you think of me?"

Merle made a noise sounding something between a sob and a groan. "I don't know! Don't change the subject. You just want to keep me stuck here. I can't do that! I say this guy is The Weaver, and even if he isn't, we've done everything anybody could expect of us. It's time to go home."

Jack, still looking as if he'd been socked in the jaw, said grimly, "I'm not going."

"All right! I'll go. You want to save the universe, fine. My dad needs me, okay? Just send me back to him!"

"Send her!" agreed Loaf, closing his eyes again. "She's giving me a headache."

Jack felt himself trembling as anger, sorrow, shock, and betrayal marched through his insides like warring armies fighting for the high ground. He struggled to keep his voice calm. "How long can it take to check this out? Just give it a little longer."

"And a little longer, and a little more after that!" Merle was beside herself. "No! I'm going home — with you or without you! Now!" With a suddenness that caught everyone by surprise, she snatched The Server.

Loaf sat up. "Hey! Cool it, Merle. Don't mess with the merchandise."

Jack clenched his fists. "Put that down, Merle!"

Bitz gave an anxious whine. "Go easy, Jack. I think Merle's a little *excited* right now. Like, the car's in drive but there's nobody at the wheel."

Help, still spinning from the force of The

Server's sudden removal by Merle, slowed to a halt, though his eyes continued to revolve. "Hey!" it protested, "not that I care, but I'm supposed to take instructions from the kid with the lousy haircut." Help gave Jack an alarmed glance. "Can we talk about this?"

"No!" Merle was beyond reason. She shook The Server. Help turned an interesting shade of green. "Set coordinates for the base."

"What base would that be?" asked Help, stalling for time.

"My dad's base," Merle said harshly. "U.S. Air Force Base, Little Slaughter, near Cambridge, England, Europe, Earth, Sol System, Rigel Sector, Milky Way Galaxy. Got it? Do you require any more information? Or should I find another exploding pine nut and ram it in your D-drive?"

"No, no," Help said hurriedly. "I get the picture."

"Good. Take me back to the day we left."

"That won't work," protested Help. "It's very dangerous because . . ."

Merle shook The Server again.

"Okay, okay!" Muttering, Help retreated. Figures flashed across the screen as the coordinates were set.

Merle gave her companions a challenging look. "I'm going home. Are you coming with me or not?"

"We're running out of runway here, Jack." Loaf hissed the words from the side of his mouth. "Do something!"

Things happened very quickly after that.

Desperately, Jack lunged toward Merle. Merle threw herself back.

At the same moment, Googie hurled herself at The Server in a frantic attempt to stop Merle.

With a flare of blue-white light, the cat and Merle both disappeared. Selenity gave a howl of terror and hid behind Loaf.

Loaf groaned. "That wasn't exactly what I had in mind."

Bitz shook his head. "This is bad. This is very bad."

"It's worse than you think." Jack's voice was shaky. "She took The Server!"

CHAPTER THREE

Cambridge District Military Protectorate
Earth, Sol System
Present day

Merle materialized on top of a crumbling pile of earth. She cried out in alarm and wind-milled her arms in an attempt to keep her balance.

Some distance away, a squat, evil-looking creature was lurching rapidly toward her. It looked like a giant turtle with a long neck. Its head swept from side to side. Smoke hung in the air behind it. As Merle watched open-mouthed, the creature gulped as if it were about to vomit. Then it gave a barking cough, and a black object flew out of its mouth straight toward Merle. Moments later, a fire-ball erupted from the ground a few yards away, instantly followed by a cloud of black smoke and a stinging hail of dirt and stones as a shattering explosion sent Merle tumbling backward. Dropping The Server, she fell with a splash into a pool of smelly, muddy water.

She rose to the surface, sputtering. "What the . . . ?"

Instantly, a strong hand was on her head, forcing her down. Shocked, Merle managed only a shallow, hurried breath before the surface closed over her again. In spite of her struggles, the hand held her under the filthy water until Merle was sure her lungs would burst.

Abruptly, the pressure eased. Merle erupted from the pool, gasping like a freshly caught fish. Even now, she was held down so that only her head stayed above the surface. A face swam into view — a face that held its finger to its lips in the universal sign for silence. Merle kept still, breathing deeply.

At length, the grip on her arms relaxed. Merle dragged herself upright. With her feet on the bottom of the pool, the scummy water reached no higher than her waist. She held her arms out and looked down in horrified disbelief at the dripping ruin of her once-fashionable clothes. She turned to face her tormentor. "Look what you did! What were you *thinking*?!"

"Where did you come from?" A young man in soaked combat fatigues stared down at Merle with a face that might have been carved out of stone. "Who are you, anyway?"

"Oh, so now you want an introduction?" Merle dropped a soggy and ironic curtsy and held her hand out. "How do you do? My name is Merle."

The young man caught his breath. Then he said, in a dead voice, "You're not Merle."

"Now, see here, mister!" Merle put her hands on her hips, in her dad's most stern manner. "You half drown me, you ruin my outfit, and then you have the nerve to tell me I don't know my own *name*? Just who do you think you are?"

The young man flinched. His voice faltered as he said, "You mean, you don't remember?"

Caught off guard, Merle shook her head. "Should I?"

The young man took a step back. "This is too much for me. Maybe you have amnesia. Maybe you're crazy."

Merle took a deep breath. What was going on? Where was she? Who was this guy and how dare he tell her she was crazy?! She snorted. "Me? Crazy? At least I don't drown people before I know their names!"

The young man shrugged impatiently. "We were being targeted by a Crawler. They have heat and motion sensors. The water masked our heat-signatures, that's why we had to lie still until it had gone."

Merle stared at him. "Do you mean that thing that shot at me?"

"Are you telling me you never saw a Crawler before?"

Merle decided to stall for time. "I guess I'm a little confused. . . ."

"I guess you are." The young man climbed out of the water and reached out to help Merle up. "Well, if you really don't remember my name — it's Lothar."

Merle stumbled, righted herself, and stared incredulously at the face of her rescuer. It was impossible, but . . . add a baseball cap, a few extra chins, flabby cheeks, and a disagreeable sneer, and he could almost be . . .

Merle's mouth dropped open with astonishment. "Loaf?"

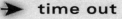

Vered II, Eridanus System
100 Gala-years ago

Selenity picked himself up off the floor. His eyes were wide-open in shock and wonder at the sight of Merle and Googie disappearing into thin air. "Cheep, Trilllll, Pertooool?" he said.

Loaf frowned. "Say what?"

The look of panic spread from Selenity's eyes to the rest of his face. He shrugged and gestured to his ears. "Prrrreeep, terwil, ptptptpt."

Loaf turned to Jack. "What's happened to the parrot's vocabulary?"

Jack shook his head. "The Server's not here, so it can't translate what he's saying. And he won't be able to understand us." Jack turned to Selenity, held his hands up, and nodded in an attempt to reassure the Veredian.

"Woof!"

"And Bitz can't talk to us, either," added Jack.

"Well, that's a good thing," quipped Loaf.

Bitz gave a deep growl and bared his teeth menacingly.

"He can still understand us, though," warned Jack.

Loaf backed away from Bitz. "Only kidding. Can't you take a joke?"

"This isn't a good time for jokes," said Jack. "We're in deep trouble. We've got to hope that Merle and Googie come back with The Server."

"And if they don't?" asked Loaf.

Jack looked grim. "If they don't, we could be stuck here forever."

The awfulness of their situation suddenly hit Loaf. No more burgers or doughnuts . . . Thoughts of a lifetime eating berries and nuts drifted through his mind. He let out a huge sigh. "Oh, that's just great."

Cambridge District Military Protectorate
Earth, Sol System
Present day

Merle stood still, searching every feature of her rescuer's face. It *was* Loaf — and yet it wasn't. It was what Loaf might look like if he hadn't spent years stuffing his face with things that were bad for him and thinking up mean schemes to get what he wanted. Lothar was a slim-jim Loaf, with muscles instead of flab, poise instead of slouch, courtesy in place of a sneer. Merle found herself wishing she wasn't dripping with water, or at least that the water had been cleaner.

She said hesitantly, "Sorry, you look like someone I know."

"Is that right?" Lothar gave a twisted smile and helped Merle scramble out of the water-logged pit. "Old blast hole," he explained, indicating their watery refuge. "From an orbital weapon. There was an air base here once." Merle looked around wildly. "Before the invasion. Nothing here now, though."

"Invasion? What invasion?"

"The invasion of the Kang." Lothar gave Merle a curious stare. "Maybe you really do have amnesia. Did you get hit on the head?"

"I forget." Merle wrung water out of her skirt.

Lothar raised his eyebrows. "Stay here, okay? I'm going to do a quick sweep of the area — make sure the coast is clear." He took an old-fashioned rifle from his shoulder, poked his head cautiously above the embankment that rose above the pit, looked around, and then belly-crawled over the lip and out of sight.

Merle knelt on the nearest thing to dry ground she could find and tried to squeeze more water out of her clothes.

"Meow?"

Merle looked up. Googie was sitting on the bank above the shell hole. Merle stared at her. "What are you doing here?"

"Meow!"

Merle gave the cat a puzzled look. Why wasn't The Server translating what Googie said? She slapped herself on the forehead. The Server! She'd had it when she arrived here. Where was it?

Merle groaned. She must have dropped it in the pool. She waded back into the scummy water. After a few moments of rummaging, she hauled out The Server and sloshed back to dry land. She opened the lid. "Help? You okay?"

Help appeared, dripping. It glared at Merle and spat out a small holographic fish that swam around Help's head, occasionally gliding in one ear and out the other.

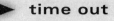

"Okay," said Merle, "you've made your point."

"Good thing this Server is guaranteed waterproof." Help burped. Bubbles appeared from the keyboard. "Mostly."

"My, my. Look what happened to you!"

Merle glared up at Googie. "Well, at least we're getting a translation again. How did you get here?"

"You dragged me along when you took off with The Server."

Merle gave a cry of dismay. "But I never meant to bring The Server with me. How did that happen?"

"You pressed the SELF-TELEPORT key while you were wrestling with the other primate," snapped Googie.

Merle groaned. "Well, at least Help is fully functional." She considered. "Let me rephrase that. It's no more dysfunctional than usual."

The hologram glared at her. "Oh, tee-hee. You slay me."

"Then would you care to tell me where we are?"

"Exactly where we should be. On Earth, your time, back at the base."

Merle turned The Server around so that Help could scan the barren landscape. Coarse grass straggled across the scorched earth in messy clumps. The sky was dull and gray, as featureless as the inside of a balloon.

"But there's no base here," Merle pointed out in an I'm-really-really-in-control sort of voice. "A guy who calls himself Lothar said there was a base here once, but there isn't anymore. He also said Earth had been invaded by the Kang, whoever they are."

Googie was staring at Merle. "The human who threw you in the pool was called Lothar? Do tell."

"Well, that's what he says. He does look a little like Loaf, except that he's kinda cute."

Googie screwed her face up. "Oh, puh-leeeease!" The cat thought for a moment. "Actually," she continued, "he might prove my theory."

"What theory?"

"My theory about where we are and how we got here. It fits all the available facts." Googie gave Merle a narrow-eyed stare. "There's one more thing I want to check. Help, get us onto the Outernet."

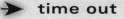

"First the mutt gives me orders," muttered Help, "now it's the fleabag." Googie hissed at it. "I'm on it! I'm on it!" the hologram said hurriedly. "We're not at home to Mister Temper, okay? I . . . uh-oh." Help's face became preoccupied.

"Uh-oh what?" snarled Googie.

For the first time, there was a look of panic on Help's sour features. "There's nothing out there!"

Googie gave a scornful sniff. "You mean you messed up making a connection?"

"I mean there's nothing to connect to!" snapped Help. "No Links, no Servers, no t-mail, no satellites, no space stations, no nothing. Zero. Zilch. Zip!"

Merle gave the hologram an uncomprehending stare. "What do you mean?"

"Petrified processors! How simple do you want this?" Help was dancing with hysteria. "There *is* no Outernet! It's gone! Vanished! Kaput! The Outernet doesn't exist!"

Googie sighed. "That proves my theory." She gazed at Merle. "I don't think you're going to like it, though."

"I don't like anything that's happened since

we arrived on Vered," Merle said miserably. "I made a fool of myself, I was mean to Jack. Since then I've been half drowned and shot at, and now you're going to tell me there's something worse?"

Googie meowed unhappily. "Much worse. Okay, here goes. I think we've hit a temporal paradox."

"Do you want to explain that?"

"Help was half right. We left the past and came to present-day Earth. But there's a problem. It isn't *our* Earth, so it isn't *our* present."

Help's holographic eyes widened. "Hey, furball! You're talking about the 'pants of time' theory, right?"

Merle said faintly, "The pants?"

"Exactly." Googie was at her most patronizing. "Every time you have a choice to make, the time stream diverges. Suppose you come across a really big pair of pants lying on the ground."

"Whose pants?"

"Nobody's pants," snapped Help. "Theoretical pants, okay?"

Merle gave an impatient shrug. "Oh, that kind. And?"

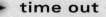

"And you have to go through them," said Googie.

"Why?"

"Never mind why, you just do!" Googie gave Merle a disgusted look. "Will you concentrate? If you choose to go down the left leg, that choice leads to a set of events. But if you choose to go down the right leg, that could lead to a completely different set of events. Get it?"

"I think so."

"All right. In our present — the present we left to go back to Vered II and meet the Dreeb kid — the Outernet exists. But we were guessing that we had to go back into the past to take The Server to The Weaver so he could create the Outernet in the first place — right?"

"Right."

"But in *this* present, the Outernet doesn't exist, because back in the past of *this* Galaxy, something happened to stop The Weaver from getting The Server, so he never created the Outernet. Is this making sense to you?"

Merle sat down very suddenly. "Oh, my . . ."

"Exactly. You flipped out and brought The

Server here, so it never got to The Weaver, so on this time line there's no Outernet and Earth has been invaded by aliens. When you lost your cool on Vered II, you wiped out our whole reality." The cat sniffed. "Honey, that is what I call a tantrum!"

"Then it's my fault?!" wailed Merle. She gazed at the waterlogged Server with an expression of guilt and horror. "I made all this happen!"

In a shower of loose dirt and rocks, Lothar slid down into the hole and landed beside her. "Who are you talking to?"

Merle quickly snapped The Server shut. ("Oh, my node!" a muffled voice protested.) "No one," she said hurriedly. "Myself."

Lothar nodded. "Shock can do that, I guess. Don't worry, I'll take you someplace safe." He looked around and shrugged. "Safer than this, anyway. Does this cat belong to you?"

Googie gave Lothar a mysterious cat stare. Merle shot her an unfriendly look. "When she feels like it. Lucky me."

"Well, it's not far to the Refuge, and there's

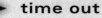

no sign of Kang patrols." Lothar climbed out of the pit.

Merle followed. "What are Kang patrols?"

Lothar gave her a puzzled look. "Where have you *been*? The Kang are the Warlord's shock troops. The invaders. You know?" Merle shook her head. Lothar rubbed his chin. "Looks like I guessed right. Amnesia. Memory loss brought on by shock. Maybe you were closer to that blast than I figured."

Merle kept her expression carefully blank. "I guess."

For more than an hour, they hiked through the broken landscape. Lothar led, his gun handy, carefully scanning the ground ahead for any signs of enemy activity. Merle followed as if in a trance. Googie brought up the rear, padding between the shell craters with feline indifference. They quickly moved over open ground cautiously where there was cover. They waded across streams and crept through marshes. Merle complained at the first one, then she decided she couldn't possibly get any wetter, and waded into the reeds. Twice they had to lie flat while distant Crawlers passed by, their scaly heads sweeping from side to side in their ruthless search.

As they went, Lothar did his best to fill in the "gaps" in Merle's memory. He "reminded" her that the Kang had invaded Earth fifty years before and, after a desperate struggle, had conquered most of the planet. There were only a few pockets of rebels left, fighting in hopeless resistance against the invading armies of the brutal nonhuman known to the conquered people of Earth as the Warlord.

At length, they arrived at a small grove of stunted, sick-looking trees. Lothar stamped a coded signal, and a tangle of brambles lifted to reveal a trapdoor. Lothar gestured for Merle to go down it. Sniffing suspiciously, Googie followed. Lothar slipped through behind them, and the trapdoor swung shut.

They were in a narrow tunnel, just high enough for Merle to walk upright. A boy, several years younger than Merle, had evidently let them in. He was carrying a candle that smoked and smelled of burning fat. He led them through the narrow passage until it opened into what looked like an underground bunker.

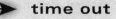

"The Brits built this in World War II." Merle jumped as Lothar's voice sounded close beside her ear. "Then the U.S. Air Force used it as an emergency command center." Lothar's face was angry and brooding in the candlelight. "Now we use it as a refuge — a sort of hideout for those of us who're still fighting the Kang."

As Merle's eyes became used to the dim light, she made out more human figures, all in combat clothing and carrying weapons. One side of the room was stacked high with boxes. Ramshackle bunks lined the other.

At a rickety desk, a powerful, dark-skinned figure sat intently studying a map by the light of an oil lamp. He looked up as Lothar and Merle approached. With a startled expression, he half rose and stood frozen, staring at the newcomer.

Merle felt tears well up in her eyes. She gave a cry, ran forward, and flung herself into the man's arms. "Dad!" She clung to him, sobbing.

But Frank Stone didn't return his daughter's embrace. Instead, he pushed her away roughly. Holding her at arm's length, he demanded hoarsely, "What is this?"

"Dad." Almost speechless with shock, Merle managed to croak, "It's me. It's Merle."

Her father gazed at her with injured, angry eyes, and his words hit her like hammer blows. "You can't be Merle. Merle is dead."

CHAPTER FOUR

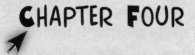

Merle scrubbed the back of her hand over her tearstained face. She was sitting, hunched against a hard stone wall, arms holding The Server between her thighs and her chest. She was in a state of confusion-overload.

Her attempts to explain herself had been cut short by the man she still thought of as her father. Frank Stone was the commander of the rebels that operated from the Refuge. He had ordered Merle to be kept in a side room while he and his lieutenants decided what to do about her.

Merle stared miserably at the activity going on in the bunker. All around, haggard-looking men and women studied maps, checked supplies, and spoke into radios. Frank Stone,

Lothar, and several other fighters were deep in heated discussion. Occasionally, there were nervous or angry glances in Merle's direction.

Googie sidled up to Merle. Checking that no one was within earshot, she sat next to her and whispered, "Remember the pant legs."

Merle stared at the chameleoid. "Googie, I don't know how familiar you are with human body language, but let me give you a few pointers. When a person curls up into the fetal position, this is not an invitation to start some stupid conversation about pants. This applies particularly to cats."

"This is a different time line from ours," said Googie, unapologetically. She nodded toward the argument going on outside. "That is not the father you know. *That* Frank Stone only exists in this reality."

Merle shook her head stubbornly. "Whatever the reality, he's still my dad. Even if he says I'm dead."

Googie arched her back. "No, he isn't. He's the other Merle's dad. His Merle died in this reality. You're not his daughter, he's not your dad."

"I know that," snapped Merle.

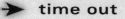

"Why don't you accept it, then?"

Merle bit her lip. "Knowing and accepting aren't the same thing. He looks like my dad, he sounds like my dad, and he's *here.*"

Googie gave a disdainful sniff. "Oh. Sentimental self-delusion. I knew you'd have a good reason."

Merle pushed the cat away. "If you want to make yourself useful, why don't you wander over there and find out what they're saying about us?"

"Who says I want to make myself useful?" Nevertheless, Googie strolled carelessly out of the door and headed toward the argument.

Seconds later, one of the men detached himself from the group around Frank Stone and headed toward Merle. He held out his hand. "What is that thing you're carrying?"

Merle clutched The Server tightly and said, "It's mine."

The man frowned. "You're in trouble, lady. That thing could be a Kang spying device. Hand it over or we'll take it."

There was no option. Reluctantly, Merle held out The Server. Moments later, the alien device that Jack had been given as a birthday present (only a few days ago, Merle realized with astonishment) was being pored over by members of the guerrilla forces. Voices were raised again as The Server failed to respond to the probing. At least Help had the sense to play dumb and stay out of sight. Even so, The Server was the subject of intense scrutiny and speculation. Clearly, even an ordinary laptop computer was a rare novelty in this reality.

Lothar left the group gathered around The Server and stepped into the room. He crouched down beside Merle and handed her a mug of thin soup. Gratefully, Merle took it. As she sipped the warm liquid, Merle was aware that she was being examined closely. Lothar was staring at her so intently that it felt as if he was trying to read her mind. She had to break the spell.

"So what does my dad say about me?"

Lothar grimaced. "He doesn't know who you are or what you are — and around here, we have enough trouble dealing with things we *do* know about. The last thing we need is something — someone — we *don't* know about!"

"Why does he think I'm dead?" asked Merle in a small voice.

Lothar's hands twitched involuntarily. "He saw the observation post where you'd been stationed after the Crawlers had gotten through with it. So did I. We knew you couldn't have survived. Of course, we never found your body." His face twisted in pain. "The post was blown to bits. We never found *anyone's* body. So I kept telling myself you might be alive, even though I knew I was fooling myself."

Tears sprang into Merle's eyes. How could she explain where she'd come from, who she really was? She turned her head away from Lothar. "So what's going to happen to me?" she asked. "I guess my dad — I mean, Frank Stone — thinks I'm a spy."

"He's not sure," replied Lothar. "He's going to talk to his wife about you. He figures that she'll be able to recognize her own daughter."

Merle's jaw dropped as shock surged through every cell in her body. "His wife . . . you mean, my mom?"

Memories flooded into her mind. Helping her mom with the baking, their hands white with flour. Bright eyes. A warm smile. Playing tennis, riding ponies on the Appalachian Trail. Photos and videos of half-remembered family events, their colors fading. Her father taking Merle out of school to tell her that her mommy had been in an accident . . .

And suddenly — miraculously — Merle might see her again. Talk to her. Hear that soft voice and feel those warm arms around her . . .

She scrambled to her feet and took Lothar's arm. "Listen, you've got to try and understand this. I need to tell you who I am and where I've come from. . . ."

She broke off. Something was happening outside. There were shouts from the rebels who had been arguing about Merle. A newcomer had joined the group — a woman who was demanding to be taken to the girl they'd just brought in.

She turned to face the room where Merle was being held, and the light from an oil lamp fell across her face.

Merle felt her mouth go dry. "Mom?"

There was a moment of absolute stillness.

Then, with a crack like a whiplash followed by a dull boom, the air in the room gathered into a fist and slammed Merle against the wall. Dust and grit fell from the ceiling. Lothar gave a yell — "They found us!" — and rushed out of the room. Merle was flung to the ground as a series of explosions rocked the bunker. She crouched in a corner, her fists clenched over her ears.

Then the ceiling came down.

Vered II, Eridanus System
100 Gala-years ago

Jack, Loaf, and Bitz had remained hidden in Selenity's room while the Veredian had headed downpole for a meal with his mother and two of his fathers. Eventually, Selenity returned, managing to sneak out a bowl of green berries and a plate of wriggling creatures that looked like a cross between maggots and cockroaches. Jack and Loaf turned down this delicacy (Jack politely, Loaf, less so) and nibbled on the berries. Bitz, however, had wolfed down the writhing goodies and now sat licking his lips contentedly.

There was still no sign of Merle, Googie, or The Server, and Loaf was becoming more and more frantic. He began pacing up and down. "Wait till I get my hands on Merle," he snarled. "How did we get into this mess? If he finds out about this, my dad's gonna kill me."

"We're on a planet several million light-years away from Earth," Jack reminded Loaf, "and about sixty years before your dad's even going to be born. He won't be able to get ahold of you."

Loaf gave Jack a glare. "You don't know my dad, he'll find a way. This whole so-called mission is just a crazy waste of time! What are we doing here?"

Jack sighed. "Trying to find The Weaver."

Loaf pointed toward Selenity. "And is *he* The Weaver?"

Jack shook his head. "I don't know. What did Janus tell us? Try to remember."

At the mention of Janus, Bitz gave a little whine. Janus was a Friends agent and former colleague of the chameleoid. He had sacrificed himself to rescue The Server from one of The Tyrant's agents. Janus had been sucked into

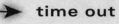

N-space, a place beyond human understanding, a universe made up of pure energy where "reality" was an optional extra.

Jack started thinking aloud. "When Janus met us in N-space, he said he had to send us back to the time he and Bitz rescued The Server — maybe even farther back. He programmed The Server to teleport us back in time and we've ended up here."

"Tell me about it!"

Jack frowned. "He wouldn't have sent us here without a good reason."

"Then why didn't he tell us what the reason was?"

Jack shrugged helplessly. "Maybe he couldn't. Maybe he didn't know, or maybe if he *did* tell us, it would change what we were going to do in some way." Jack looked across at Selenity and gave him a crooked smile. The Veredian returned a beaky grin. "That reason may have something to do with Selenity, I guess. Perhaps there's some information in The Server that Selenity can use."

"But it isn't here anymore," growled Loaf. "Thanks to Merle."

Jack thought for a second or two. "Maybe Selenity's computer is the key to this. Maybe it could get us back to Earth."

Loaf gave a snort of ridicule. "That thing? It makes my windup Mickey Mouse clock look modern."

Jack ignored Loaf's complaints. He nodded toward Selenity's computer and mimed typing on the keyboard, "Selenity, show me what your computer can do."

Cambridge District Military Protectorate
Alternate Earth, Sol System
Present day

"Merle! Merle! Are you okay? Talk to me!"

Lothar's frantic cries roused Merle. The room was half full of rubble. She was covered in dust. Her head ached. Groggily, she struggled to her knees. "I'm here!"

"The Kang have stopped bombing. They'll send ground forces in any minute now. We're using the emergency exits." Lothar's voice was harsh. "But there's a ton of debris blocking you in there. We can't get you out!"

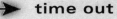

Merle's head cleared. "Don't try! There's no time! Are my mom and dad okay?"

"Yes. Frank's leading the escape. Your . . . mom . . . is with him."

"And you still have The Server?"

"That box of yours? Sure, but what . . ."

"Just keep it safe, okay? And Googie? My cat?"

"Yeah, she's out here, too. Crazy animal keeps trying to dig through to you."

In spite of her pain and fear, Merle felt relief come over her. "Take her and The Server and get away. There's nothing you can do for me."

Lothar swore violently. "Guess you're right. I can't do you any good if I'm dead. Okay, I'm out of here. But I promise I'll come back for you. You hear me?"

"I hear you! Now get out of here!"

"Whatever it takes, I'll come back! Hold that thought!" There was a scuffle, then silence.

Merle sat for a long time in the suffocating darkness, alone with her thoughts. She knew that she had only herself to blame for this mess. Would she get to meet her mom?

Would Lothar really come back for her? How could she get back to Jack and the others? Was she going to die here?

At last, noises filtered down into her prison. Thuds and the grinding sound of concrete slabs being lifted.

And then, with a final flood of loose earth, part of the ceiling was lifted away, admitting a blinding light and harsh, alien voices speaking an unknown language.

Then a human voice rang out. "Anyone down there?"

Merle scrambled to her feet.

"Anyone there?!"

Licking her dry, dust-smeared lips, Merle called, "Lothar?" in little more than a whisper.

"Come out slowly. No sudden moves. Keep your hands where I can see them."

Merle scrambled through the gap and stood blinking in the light. Facing her was a human figure with dark spiky hair. Merle recognized him immediately.

"Jack!" Merle gave a sob of relief. "You got here! You found me! I'm sorry I did what I did, but you won't believe what happened. I saw my mom and I've met another Loaf, only this one is incredible, he's totally different from the Loaf we know, and . . . this is a different reality and . . ."

Merle's voice trailed off. Jack wasn't dressed in the messy clothes she'd last seen him wearing. His black uniform was immaculate.

"Jack?"

Jack stared at her with a mixture of confusion and hatred. He leveled a deadly-looking weapon at Merle.

"I don't know how you know my name, and I don't know who you are. But if you know the traitor called Lothar, you are a rebel and an enemy."

"What have you got there, Section-Leader Armstrong?" A smooth, hissing, wicked-sounding voice spoke from somewhere behind Merle.

Jack immediately snapped to attention. "A rebel fugitive, Warlord, trapped by our bombardment."

Merle turned and choked back a cry of horror at the familiar, six-armed elephant-eared figure who sat easily in a floating chair. She managed to find her voice. "Tracer!"

The creature, who in Merle's reality had been The Tyrant's evil chief of surveillance, gazed at her as if she were some species of animal that had just performed an unexpected but not very interesting trick.

Merle spun around, her arms open wide in appeal, and wailed, "Jack!"

Jack shot her.

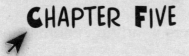CHAPTER FIVE

Vered II, Eridanus System
100 Gala-years ago

Selenity's mom finished shouting at her unfortunate son and, with a parting, "Wait till your fathers get home," disappeared down the climbing pole muttering that if she'd known how much trouble Selenity would be, she'd have dropped him out of the tree while he was still an egg. She'd just discovered the fate of the vidi-books.

The vine curtains in front of Selenity's closet parted and Bitz peered out cautiously. Jack and Loaf crawled out from under Selenity's bed, half-suffocated and smelling of leaf mold.

Jack brushed at his leaf-stained pants. "That was too close. If Merle doesn't get here soon, the Veredians are going to find us, and we're going to wind up in some kind of freak show."

"Or," said Loaf gloomily, "in some lab." He rubbed a bruised shin. "Probably in jars."

Selenity's computer made a beeping noise. Koffkoff's reply to the message Selenity had sent before his mother's unexpected arrival had come through.

Loaf checked his watch and snorted. "Eleven minutes to get a message to the next planet and back! And you think this thing can take us to Earth? Ha!" Loaf shook his head. "We've seen e-mail, o-mail, and t-mail, but this thing has d-mail. *D* as in dinosaur. It's useless!"

It pained Jack to agree with Loaf's assessment, but he had no choice. He, Loaf, and Bitz were stuck. Only Merle and The Server could rescue them.

Headquarters of the Warlord
Alternate Earth, Sol System
Present day

Merle awoke to find herself strapped into a chair with Tracer's repellent figure looming

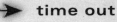

over her. "Get your paws off me!" she snapped. "And the other four!"

Jack stepped forward to stand by Tracer. "It is not wise to speak to the Warlord in such a fashion."

"Warlord?" Merle gave Tracer a look of absolute loathing. Then she glared at Jack. "You shot me!" she complained.

"So he did." Tracer gave Jack a thin smile. "With an energy pistol set to stun, the old softy!" Jack's face remained expressionless. "However," Tracer continued, "my lieutenant's uncharacteristic act of mercy does give me the opportunity to interrogate you about your rebel associates. I warn you, my patience is not great." The creature gave Merle an evil grin. "What am I saying? I haven't any patience at all! Torturer!" The Warlord sat down and drummed with the fingers of six hands, regarding Merle with hooded eyes. Eyes?! Merle shook herself. The Tracer in her reality had no eyes. The Tyrant's Chief of Surveillance could "see" only by using a virtual-reality visor.

Merle had no more time for thought. Jack snapped his fingers. A flat-headed being, oozing viciousness and slime in equal amounts, came forward.

"Earthling," the disgusting creature slobbered, "prepare to meet your worst nightmare."

"Halt!" The Warlord was on his feet, eyes blazing. "Aren't we forgetting something?"

The interrogator gazed at its master in dismay. "Ooops. Sorry, O Wicked One." It turned back to Merle. "I have to explain what I'm going to do to you, don't I? Or you won't be crying with terror when I do it, because you won't know what to expect, and that would never do . . ."

"Hurry up!" The angry Warlord reached for a tub of something resembling popcorn. He held this in two hands and began stuffing his face with three more. With his sixth hand he pointed at the interrogator. "This creature is a Kippan chameleoid," he snarled. "Currently, it has taken the form of a Molassian seeping toad. But at my command, it will drive you crazy with terror by turning itself into creatures from the deepest and darkest corners of your nightmares."

"Awwww!" groaned the interrogator. "I wanted to say that."

The Warlord gave the creature a furious glare. The interrogator cringed, then turned its attention back to Merle. "Prepare yourself, human. Unimaginable horrors await you, unless you answer the question."

Merle gritted her teeth. "What question?"

The interrogator clicked its drooling jaws. "Sorry. I'll probably forget my own heads next time." It turned to the Warlord. "What question do you wish to ask, Lord?"

The Warlord waved irritably. "I don't know! Just turn into something horrible."

The interrogator shook its heads sorrowfully. "Can't do that without a question, my Lord. That's the rules."

The Warlord gave a theatrical sigh. Jack stepped to his master's side. "Perhaps, my Lord, she can tell us the rebels' escape plans." The Warlord nodded eagerly.

"Right, Your Lordship!" The interrogator gave Merle a horrifying grin. "All right, Earthscum, tell me where your rebel friends went, or I shall turn into something unspeakable." It

85

leaned closer and whispered, "What are you most afraid of?"

Merle gave it an incredulous look. "What?"

"Well, you're my first victim from Earth. I don't know what to turn into that will scare you the most. Please tell me or His Wickedness will get really mad." The interrogator glanced over its shoulder at the angry Warlord and cringed. "You don't want me to get in trouble, do you?"

Merle said thoughtfully, "Well, I'm really scared of kittens."

The interrogator blinked. "Kittens? Are you sure?"

Merle nodded eagerly. "Oh, yes. Especially the cuddly, fluffy kind. They're really scary."

"All right!" The Kippan pulled itself up. "Then I will turn myself into a fearful, terrifying . . . kitten!"

The chameleoid changed into an adorable longhaired Persian Blue kitten with big round eyes. Merle immediately went into a well-acted screaming tantrum. "Oh, no! It's cute! Aaaargh! It's going to rub against me with its horrible soft fur! Oh, nooooo!"

Unfortunately for Merle, the Warlord was

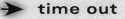

not fooled. Jumping to his feet (and spilling his snack), the enraged being screamed at the pathetic kitten. "Fool! Idiot! Incompetent worm! Can't you see she's pretending?" The Warlord gave Merle an evil grin. "Very sneaky, Earth-creature, but it won't save you." He turned back to the Kippan. "Turn yourself into the eyeball-popping razor-toothed ear-driller from the planet Aaaaaargh! No life-form can handle such a threat!"

Merle bit her lip. Googie once threatened Loaf with the eyeball-popping razor-toothed ear-driller from the planet Aaaaaargh! She didn't make it sound like this was a creature you'd find in a petting zoo.

The kitten began to change. Merle's eyes widened as the Kippan re-formed its body into a being so disgusting, so indescribably monstrous . . .

Merle lost her nerve. She closed her eyes and screamed.

"Merle!"

Merle looked up into the concerned face of Lothar. He had a strip of rag tied around his forehead and was carrying a whole armory of lethal weapons.

"Oh, there you are." Googie looked up from The Server and gave a dainty sniff. "Nice adventure you led me on."

Merle realized she was no longer strapped to a chair. She was in a steel-lined corridor, and Tracer, Jack, and the Torturer had gone. "Where am I?"

"I teleported you here," said Googie matter-of-factly. "It wasn't easy. We had to go right into the Warlord's headquarters before we could get a good fix on you. There's some kind of shield. Not that Mister Muscles here minded. He was all for storming the Warlord's command center, all by himself."

Merle stared at Lothar. "But how did you get in here? Isn't it guarded?"

Lothar showed her a scary-looking weapon. "It *was*." Merle looked past his shoulder. There was a haze of smoke farther down the corridor and several crumpled shapes.

"You mean, you came in here with guns blazing to try to rescue me?" Merle said blankly. "Don't think I'm ungrateful, but don't you think that was . . . kinda macho?"

"She means stupid," Googie translated helpfully.

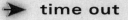

Lothar shrugged. "I said I'd come back for you. Anyhow, after the Refuge was overrun, I lost touch with the others. Then I found the cat . . ."

"What he means," said Googie dryly, "is that *I* found *him.*"

"And she said, 'We've got to rescue Merle,' and I said, 'Hey, you're talking!' and she said, 'Haven't you ever seen a talking cat before?' And I said, 'Now that you mention it, no.' And she said . . ."

"Are we having a conversation," Googie demanded of no one in particular, "or are we escaping?"

Merle looked up and down the corridor. "The Warlord will come whooping and hollering after me any second now." She stared Lothar straight in the eyes. "Listen, I can get us out of here. I can make all this right. I can make it so it never happened." She picked up The Server as she spoke. "And you're coming with me, right?"

Lothar stared at Merle. "I guess that bang on the head really shook a few screws loose. This is crazy talk."

Merle stamped her foot in exasperation.

"You don't understand! I'm going to go back in time."

Lothar nodded gravely. "Sure you are."

"I'm not joking! Listen to me! When I go back, this whole reality will probably cease to exist! What I have to do will change the course of history. The Warlord won't exist. Neither will Dad or . . . Mom." Merle's eyes filled with tears. "Neither will you. You've got to come with me!"

"I don't *have* to do anything." Lothar had started to back away. "You're crazy."

Merle choked back a sob. "I thought you liked me."

"Liked you?!" Lothar's explosive cry jolted Merle so much that she nearly dropped The Server. "Liked you? Before you . . . died, we were . . . I mean, you were . . . that is . . ." Lothar's face was a mask of grief. "Don't you remember?"

Merle felt her cheeks burning beneath the tears that rolled down them. "That wasn't me. I'm sorry."

The clatter of running footsteps echoed down the corridor. Lothar dropped into a crouch and prepared to fire. "Get going. I'll cover you."

"There are too many of them! They'll blow you to bits!"

"Maybe." Lothar grinned savagely. "Eventually."

He stared down the corridor. Merle stood fuming for a moment, then tapped a return command into The Server and pressed the SEND key.

By the time the Warlord's guards skidded into the corridor, their prey was no more than three indistinct blue-white outlines, shapes that hung for a moment in the empty air and then faded to nothingness.

Vered II, Eridanus System
100 Gala-years ago

Loaf looked up with a scowl as flashes of blue-white light shot around Selenity's bedroom. He glared at Merle and Googie. "Boy, you sure took your time!" Then he spotted Lothar, and his jaw dropped. "Who's the beefcake?"

"You shouldn't have done that, Merle," said Lothar.

Bitz barked joyously. Jack flung his arms around Merle, then hastily released her. "We thought . . . we thought you weren't coming back."

Loaf regarded Lothar with sullen suspicion. Lothar looked Jack up and down.

Selenity said, "I can understand you again!" Hearing the alien voice, Lothar whipped the largest of his guns around and pointed it at the Veredian, who gave a squeak of dismay and dived headfirst through the window. Tig climbed to a high shelf, chirping with rage, and threw things at the astonished human.

Jack and Merle exchanged glances. Jack said, "Maybe we'd all better sit down. We've got a lot of catching up to do. I guess we're in for a long night."

When Merle had finished describing her adventures, Jack sat for a while with his chin resting on his hands, lost in thought.

Loaf was gazing at Lothar in horrified fascination. "He went up against hundreds of heavily armed guards? Alone? To save *you*?" Loaf shook his head. "Man! What a sap!"

Lothar had been watching Loaf closely. Now he turned to Merle and said, "Have I got this right? You're saying that, in your reality,

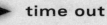

I'm . . . *him*?" He gave Loaf a look of utter disgust.

"I'm not you, hotshot!" snarled Loaf. "Let's get that clear right now, okay? I'm not some muscle-bound hunk who thinks he's Rambo. I'm *me*!"

Lothar shook his head gravely. "Tough break," he said, just loudly enough to be heard.

"Oh, yeah?"

"All right!" Jack stood up decisively. "We don't have time for fighting. We did enough of that when we arrived here and nearly blew the mission."

"*I* nearly blew the mission, you mean," said Merle glumly.

Jack shook his head. "You were right all along."

Merle gave him a blank stare. "Excuse me?"

"You wanted to download The Server's knowledge into Selenity's computer from the beginning." Jack shrugged. "I'm still not sure it's what Janus wanted us to do, but right now it looks to me like our only option."

Bitz gave a yap of agreement. "If we have

The Server take us forward in time with things as they are, we'll just end up in the reality Merle just left — and this time, we might not be as lucky as she was. We might get captured or killed. We might lose The Server. Either way, it'll be curtains for *our* reality."

"Maybe not. But Merle brought Lothar here against his will." Jack turned to Lothar. "Do you want to go back?"

Lothar looked at Merle and said nothing.

"The way I see it," said Googie, "in the alternate reality we traveled to, the Galaxy had no Outernet to pull it together, so I guess life-forms evolved at different rates. No Weaver, no Tyrant, no Friends, no FOEs, just lots of little local wars with stronger species enslaving weaker ones."

Jack nodded. "We don't know what Janus wanted us to do. So we have to do what we think is right." Jack motioned to Selenity, who was sitting as far away from Lothar's guns as possible. Hesitantly, Selenity came forward.

Jack handed The Server to the young Veredian. "Selenity, I don't know whether you are The Weaver, and I know you didn't ask to be

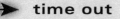

involved in this." Jack looked around at his companions and smiled crookedly. "None of us did. But somewhere along the line, a decision has to be made. Help will download what you need to know to get the Outernet going. Then, I'm afraid, it's up to you."

Selenity took The Server with honor.

Googie eyed Selenity's computer doubtfully. "Are you sure that machine of yours has enough memory for this?"

"You bet it does." Selenity, already rummaging around the back of his machine, looked up proudly. "This box of bits may be slow, but I built it with tons of memory." He gave a squeal of excitement as The Server obligingly popped out a socket to fit the connector from Selenity's machine.

Jack turned to Merle. "Will you start the download?"

Silent tears rolled down Merle's cheeks. She turned to Lothar. "Once I've done this, my dad will no longer exist in your reality. My mom won't exist in *either* reality. You can never go home again."

"I haven't had a home in a long time," said

Lothar slowly. "If Earth is still free in this real-ity, then your reality is better than mine. In any case, I guess this is something you have to do." He shrugged. "So do it."

Behind Lothar's back, Loaf mimed sticking his fingers down his throat.

Merle tapped at The Server's keyboard. Se-lenity nodded as a line of indecipherable code appeared on his computer screen. "It's down-loading."

Jack put his hand on the Veredian's shoul-der. "Selenity, as soon as the download is complete, we'd better go." Selenity turned to him, startled, and made a small sound of dis-tress. Jack held up his hand. "We have to. We've had some close calls as it is. Your mom would end up finding us sooner or later. Any-way, you've got plenty to do. With the infor-mation you're downloading right now, you'll be able to show your people how to communi-cate across all your colony worlds. Across the whole Galaxy, too, one day."

Selenity nodded miserably. Putting his beak close to Jack's ear, he said, "To tell you the truth, Jack, I'm not sure I'm up to it."

In return, Jack whispered, "To tell you the

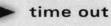

truth, Selenity, that's exactly how I felt when The Server ended up in my lap."

Selenity gave him a startled look. "But you seem so sure about what you're doing."

Jack gave him a sympathetic grin. "Good act, huh?" He turned to Lothar. "Will you join us? We need all the help we can get." He held out his hand.

After a moment's hesitation, Lothar took it. Loaf glowered.

There was a beeping from Selenity's computer. The Veredian checked his screen. "That's it. Download complete, and it's backed up automatically."

"Then I suppose this is good-bye." Jack turned to Merle. "We need to set up the teleport to our own time . . ." His voice trailed off as Merle shook her head. Her shoulders were shaking.

"Oh, for crying out loud!" Loaf snatched The Server. "I'll do it."

Jack looked at him uncertainly. "Are you sure you can . . . ?"

"What's *your* problem?" demanded Loaf harshly. "Why does *she* have to do everything? You think I can't set a few dumb coordinates? So what do I get to do around here now that the blue-eyed boy has shown up?" He jerked a thumb at Lothar. "What you got me down for, Jack? Carrying the luggage?"

"Okay, okay." Jack held up his hands. "Set the coordinates."

Tig skittered over to Merle and climbed onto her shoulder, patting her moist cheek and crooning worriedly. Merle nuzzled Tig's soft fur and managed a weak smile as she handed him back to Selenity. "Sorry. You didn't see me at my best."

Selenity shuffled his feet. "Gee, that's okay." Merle kissed him on the beak, and he turned bright green in embarrassment. "Gosh."

Bitz put his paws on Selenity's shoulders and licked his face. Jack shook hands in farewell — after some confusion — as the Veredian custom seemed to be to shake both right hands simultaneously.

"Are we leaving now?" demanded Loaf. "Or what?"

Jack gave Selenity a last wave of farewell and stepped back to join his companions. Loaf's finger jabbed down on the SEND key . . .

. . . and in a flare of blue-white light, they were gone.

**U.S. Air Force Base, Little Slaughter,
near Cambridge, England
Earth, Sol System
Present day**

They materialized in the middle of a war zone.

Strange boomerang-shaped crafts tore the air to shreds above them. Bombs and missiles rained down. Energy beams torched trees and turned acres of soil into dirty glass. Black clouds rumbled in the tormented sky. The earth heaved and shook.

The companions lay on the ground watching in horror as the U.S. Air Force Base was pulverized. Battalions of Bugs, The Tyrant's most feared troops, advanced toward groups of fleeing humans. Heavy guns coughed nearby, pounding more distant targets. As far as the companions could see, not a building was left standing.

Jack's voice shook. "Is this really *our* Earth?"

But Merle wasn't looking at the carnage be-

fore them. She was casting her eyes desperately around the small group of companions,
searching for a face that wasn't there.

With her heart freezing within her, she said,
"Where's Lothar?"

CHAPTER SIX

U.S. Air Force Base, Little Slaughter, near Cambridge, England
Alternate Earth 2, Sol System
Present day

Merle gave a howl of fury and threw herself at Loaf, fists flying. "You left him behind!"

Loaf dropped The Server and crouched, his head tucked into his arms, in a desperate attempt to ward off Merle's attack. "Get her off me! She's crazy! She's trying to kill me!"

One of the boomerang-shaped crafts screamed overhead. Violent explosions tore up the ground all around them.

"She's not the only one!" Jack rubbed dirt out of his eyes. "This looks like the base — the layout is the same — but this sure wasn't happening when we left! Anyone know who's shooting at us?"

"FOEs," snarled Bitz. "Those are Decimator ground-attack fighters. Standard invasion tactics: landing of shock troops backed up by alr cover."

"FOEs? Invading Earth? Merle, leave him alone!" Jack grabbed the furious girl's shoulders. "Calm down!"

Googie had a mouthful of Merle's clothing and was tugging hard and growling cat oaths under her breath, until she spat out the cloth and said, "Yes, calm down! What's the matter with you? You made me snag a claw! Do you know how much that *hurts*?"

Merle was shaking with fury as they dragged her away from Loaf. "Calm down nothing!" Loaf uncurled, took one look at Merle's expression, and scrambled backward. "Lothar came back for me! He came *back*! And you stranded him on an alien world a hundred years ago!"

"Maybe it was an accident!" said Jack desperately. "Listen!" Merle's struggles eased up for a moment. "Maybe the coordinates don't allow two people who are really one person to be teleported. Or maybe someone from a different time line *couldn't* be teleported into this one."

Merle made another lunge at Loaf. "Or

maybe the traitorous slimeball who set the co-ordinates deliberately fixed it so Lothar didn't come with us!"

Another FOEs craft zeroed in on their position. The companions threw themselves onto the ground. The solid earth buckled beneath them as a series of titanic explosions showered them with debris.

Jack looked up, shaking his head, dazed. "I don't get it! Why are the FOEs attacking Earth?"

Bitz gave a sharp whine. "That's why!"

Jack followed the dog's gaze and gave a cry of horror.

Two familiar figures were racing through the ruins of the air force base, hurdling bomb craters, dodging the burning wrecks of aircraft and vehicles. One was a lean, athletic-looking man, and the other was a mongrel dog with a messy coat.

"That's me!" yapped Bitz. "And Janus! The FOEs must have followed us here!"

Merle forgot temporarily about trying to kill Loaf. "But in *our* reality you rescued The Server and had enough time for Janus to lead the FOEs away from Earth."

Googie nodded. "So this must be yet *another* time line where you *didn't* manage to save The Server, but you still ended up here."

"Never mind that!" snapped Bitz. "We've got to help us . . . I mean them!" The dog stood on its hind legs, waving its forepaws for balance. "Hey, Janus! Over here."

He got no farther. A shattering explosion pulverized the earth where the fugitives had been running. Once again, Jack and his friends were thrown to the ground. When they picked themselves up, Janus and his companion were nowhere to be seen.

Bitz howled. "Come on! We've gotta save them!"

"No, Bitz! Stop!" Jack's voice was harsh. "They couldn't have survived that blast!"

"You don't know that! We can't just leave . . ."

"Listen!" Jack knelt by the agitated dog and took Bitz's face between his hands. "Whether they survived or not, nothing we can do here and now will help them, or us, or Earth. It's too late for that!"

Googie touched noses with Bitz. "Jack's

right. Whatever went wrong happened in the recent past. Probably when you tried to take The Server from Vered. If we're to wipe out this time line and get our own reality back on track, that's where we've got to go!"

Merle marched over to Loaf, who backed away. Merle contented herself with a nasty look, and snatched The Server from his hands. "Agreed. But first, we go back to Selenity's time to get Lothar."

Jack held Bitz's gaze. "Okay?"

Bitz's ears drooped. He gave a despairing whine. In a barely audible voice, he said, "Okay. This is a lousy reality, anyway."

Jack looked around at the circling attack-craft and the approaching Bugs. "Then let's go. And make it quick."

Merle nodded. Her hands shook as she typed in the return coordinates for Vered. With a final glance at the raging apocalypse before them, she hit the SEND key.

Immediately, a blue-white vortex spiraled from The Server and engulfed all five Friends. They faded from existence, leaving only out-lines in the dust-filled air.

Moments later, the ground where they had been standing erupted as a FOEs weapon finally targeted the intruders . . .

. . . but, for The Tyrant's ambitions, too late.

N-Space

The roaring of the t-t-event vortex ceased and Jack found himself standing still in a universe of movement. Particles of light streamed all around him, shimmering and glowing, morphing into many different shapes and patterns. He felt a shock of dislocation: This certainly wasn't Vered II!

Jack sensed the presence of his companions. He turned his head and could make out their ghostlike outlines. Currents of energy pulsed through their transparent bodies, giving them the appearance of three-dimensional ultrasound images captured by a giant body-scanner.

Jack felt a reassuring knowledge surge through his mind.

N   S   p   a   c   e.

They were back in the strange universe of pure energy, where the past, present, and fu-

ture met. It was a place beyond human understanding, a place where normal senses were
useless. They had been here before.

Suddenly, the movement around Jack
ceased.

Jack blinked in shock at his new surroundings. The companions were standing in a
barn. Bales of hay were scattered all around. A
rusting wheelbarrow leaned against one of
the corrugated metal walls. Bags of animal
feed were stacked high, and in the middle of
the barn, on a hay bale, sat a bald-headed, humanoid figure.

"Janus!" Bitz gave a yowl of joy and
rushed over to his friend.

"This isn't real. We're in N-space again,
aren't we?" asked Loaf.

Janus's yellow eyes sparkled. "To enable
us to communicate in a world you understand,
I've again created familiar surroundings from
the memory of one of you."

"Mine," said Jack. "It's our old barn. When
Dad had the farm. I used to spend hours in it."
He looked around, taking in the details. It was
exactly as he remembered it. Except that it
wasn't real. Outside the barn, the kaleidoscope

of energy particles oscillated, converged, and diverged in an ever-changing cosmic dance.

"Janus," said Jack, "we gave Selenity the information he needed to start the Outernet. Is that what you wanted?" Janus nodded. "Then why didn't you tell us that's what we had to do?"

Janus shook his head. "I didn't dare. If I had, the outcome of your visit might have been different. I could not take the risk."

"Risk?" Merle bore down on Janus, fuming with impatience. "It seems to me that we've been taking *all* the risks. Anyway, why have you brought us here? We have to get back to Vered and rescue Lothar."

Janus held up a hand. Merle was silenced. "I know where you planned to go, and why," he said. "That is why I intercepted your t-mail and brought you here."

Janus gazed into Merle's angry eyes. His expression was grave. "In the reality you have just visited, Sirius and I were unable to stop The Server from falling into the hands of the FOEs. With the last remaining Server in his possession, The Tyrant is making good on his threats to bring the whole Galaxy under his domination. On that time line, Earth is just one of hundreds of planets being overrun by the FOEs even as we speak.

"And his rule of terror will continue for as long as that time line exists," continued Janus. "Until you erase it and restore the reality you know, billions will suffer throughout the Galaxy."

"So what do we have to do?" asked Jack.

"As you have already guessed, you must return to Vered."

Merle clenched her fists. "Then why . . . ?"

". . . did I bring you here?" Janus gave Merle a compassionate look. "Because the Vered you must go to is not the Vered you have just left. Your mission to Selenity's time is complete."

Merle glared at Janus in disbelief. "But what about Lothar? He came back for me, I have to go back for him. I can't leave him there!"

"You must." Janus's voice was relentless.

Merle's eyes flashed. "Why?"

Janus shook his head wearily. "I cannot tell you why. There are wheels within wheels, and realities within realities."

"Don't give me that mumbo jumbo!" snapped Merle. "Why should I leave Lothar behind just because you say so? What do you know?!"

Janus looked up, and the pain in his catlike eyes silenced Merle. "What do I know? Be thankful that you do not bear the burden of what I know!" Janus turned away and when he spoke again his voice was calm and sad. "I can tell you nothing more. You must return to Vered at the time when Sirius and I traced The Server there, before we came to your Earth a little more than a year ago. Your task now is to help Sirius and me rescue The Server on Vered II."

Bitz whined at the mention of his code name. "Gee, Janus, I know you can see things from here that we can't see, but how do you figure that? If we — they — helped us — them . . . I mean . . ."

"I think I can explain what this drooling mutt is trying to say," purred Googie. Bitz growled at her.

"When he and Janus came to Vered to rescue The Server, they didn't see us and we didn't help them. So if they see us, or we help them *now,* that will just send us off into *another* different reality."

"That is why, at all costs, you must not allow Sirius or me to see you."

"So we have to fight off hordes of Bugs and rescue you, but you can't know anything about it?" Googie shook her head. "Well, isn't that just dandy?"

Merle gave Janus a look of pure loathing. "Why should we help you?"

Jack turned to Merle and gripped her shoulders firmly. "Merle, I'm sorry about Lothar. I really am. But if we're going to get back to our own reality, we're going to need you. Please?"

Merle glared at Jack. Then, slowly, she lowered her eyes. Almost unnoticed, she nodded.

"Then let's go," said Loaf. He pointed at Merle. "Just keep her off my back!"

Jack swung menacingly around to face him. "The jury's still out on you. Your best bet is to do exactly what you're told and say as little as possible."

Loaf opened his mouth to make a snappy

comeback — then he saw the looks he was getting from his companions and thought better of it. His mouth closed with a snap.

Jack turned to Janus. "I guess we're ready."

"Then it is time for you to go. Good luck. The future of the Galaxy rests on your shoulders. Not one of you has chosen this burden, but if the Galaxy is to survive, all of you must bear it." Solemnly, Janus made the secret sign of the Friends.

The barn vanished in a flash of blue and white as the five companions tumbled helplessly once more through time and space.

Vered II, Eridanus System, Eclipse Sector
One year ago

They rematerialized in a huge, square room crammed with machinery. Around and above them, metal gleamed in the dim light admitted by four huge translucent, circular windows. As his eyes adjusted to the light, Jack realized that they were standing in the midst of a giant clockwork mechanism. Throughout the huge space, wheels spun, springs unwound, cogs clicked, regulators whirred, and shafts turned.

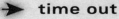 **time out**

Merle was the first to say aloud where they'd emerged. "We're in a clock!"

"The Great Clock of Vered II," said Bitz. "The clock that has no numbers!" He explained the Veredians' curious attachment to time.

"So these big windows are the clock faces." Merle gazed at the dials, and her brow creased. "But these faces have numbers. I can't read them, they're in Veredian, but . . ."

"What does that mean?" asked Jack uneasily. "Is this the wrong clock?"

Bitz shook his head. "Nope. This is the clock, all right. This is how it looked last time I was here. The FOEs put the numbers there. Slaves of The Tyrant need to know what time it is."

Loaf was staring out through a hole in one of the cracked and discolored clock faces. Hundreds of feet below him lay Green Square and the surrounding city. "Hey, guys," he murmured. "You should see this."

Jack and the chameleoids scrambled up to join Loaf. Merle followed more slowly and stood as far away from Loaf as possible.

Far below, a squad of ten black-shirted,

leather-booted Veredians marched across the square. One of the group carried a large black banner with a white symbol — two clenched fists — in its center. They stomped across the square, eyes resolutely forward, then marched down a side street and disappeared into the distance.

Bitz gave a snarl of disgust. "Curfew patrol. I met up with a group of similar goons when I was here with Janus." Bitz shivered. "And I gotta tell you, it's not in my top ten all-time-favorite moments."

"They remind me of those thugs that attacked Selenity," said Jack. "Didn't he call them the Hard Fists or something?"

Bitz growled. "They're the boss beings around here. Been in league with The Tyrant for years."

Merle frowned. "You're telling me that those thugs we scared off when we rescued Selenity became rulers of this planet?"

"Seems like it. We should have really taught them a lesson when we first met up with them," said Bitz. "That might have changed things."

"I think we've changed history quite enough for one day," said Googie primly.

"Do you think Selenity will still be around?" asked Merle.

"He's probably dead," replied Jack. "Remember, we met him a hundred years ago."

"I hate to cut in on the reminiscing," said Googie, "but we have a mission, remember?"

A low hiss from Loaf cut across Jack's reply. "Hey! Look over here! Those Hard Fist guys aren't the only bad guys we have to worry about."

Jack looked downward. At first, he saw nothing. Then dark gray shapes detached themselves from the shadows and broke into a lumbering run across the square.

Jack swore under his breath. "Bugs!"

CHAPTER SEVEN

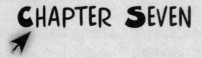

Bitz clambered up beside Jack and planted his paws on the broken plastic of the clock face, watching the scene below. He nodded. "Figures. We knew they were looking for The Server, too."

Jack looked across the square to the city beyond and gave a whistle. "If this is Vered, where have all the trees gone?"

"It's Vered, all right," said Bitz unhappily. "Just like it was when Janus and me rescued The Server. See what happens to a planet after years of being ruled by the FOEs?" Bitz shook his head sadly. "No wonder I didn't recognize it when we met Selenity."

The tree in which the clock sat was withered and leafless. It had died long ago. In fact, most of the trees of Vered City were gone, replaced by drab concrete buildings that fell away beneath them to vanish in the thick, greasy vapor that seethed and coiled above the invisible forest floor. Some trees grew among the featureless gray structures, but there was no sign of the thick forests that had greeted the companions a hundred years ago.

Jack turned away from the ruined vista. "Let's just do what we have to do and get out of here. Bitz, where's the Veredian Server?"

Bitz turned to face the clock. "Right here."

"What do you mean," asked Googie sweetly, " 'right here'?"

Bitz had clearly been asking himself the same question. He scanned the room frantically. "Right here! At least, it should be. This is where it was!"

"Well, it's not here now."

"I can see that!" snapped Bitz. "I don't understand it! It was right here . . ."

Googie gave an exasperated sigh. "Typical! Come on, think. Cast your mind, such as it is, back. You came here to find the lost Server of Vered . . ."

Bitz nodded, his face screwed up in concentration. "Yeah. When the FOEs invaded Vered, they never found its Server. They assumed Friends who'd escaped took it with them, but we knew we didn't have it. We thought it had been destroyed in the invasion. Then, when we lost our last Server to The Tyrant, we started to hear rumors that the missing Server had been hidden somewhere on Vered *time beyond reckoning.* I was sent on a seek-and-find mission. Got a ride on some cargo ship here and shape-shifted to fit in with the local population."

"What happened?"

"I got caught by the FOEs — the Hard Fists. Just a bunch of thugs. Turned out, they also wanted to know where the missing Server was, so they sent me down to their torture chambers for a session of Twenty Questions with lots of screaming in between." Bitz shuddered. "Good thing Janus got to me before the Bugs got there to do their worst."

"And?"

"Janus disobeyed orders from his commander. Don't know how he found out where I

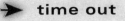

was, but he teleported to Vered and got me out of the FOEs clutches. I owe him my life . . . or, at least, the fact that most of my body parts are still in good working order."

Merle took a deep breath. "Like Lothar rescued me. I know how you feel."

"One little mistake," whined Loaf. "Are you going to hold it against me forever?"

Merle's eyes were diamond-hard and unforgiving. "No. Longer than that."

"Don't interrupt!" snapped Bitz. "I'm remembering! Janus figured he'd solved the clue. *Time beyond reckoning,* get it? He found out that when it was built, this clock had no numbers. He figured The Server must be hidden here. Nobody can reckon time on a clock with no numbers.

"So we made our way up here, found The Server, and teleported to Earth with the FOEs in hot pursuit, and the rest you know."

"Finally, we get to the point!" said Googie. "So you found The Server. What does it look like?"

"It's a crystal, okay? About the size of a basketball, and glowing."

Merle pointed up into the mechanism above their heads. "You mean, like the one up there?"

Bitz looked up, and his jaw dropped open. "That looks like it, all right. But it wasn't up there, it was down here!"

"Sure it was." Googie gave Bitz a superior smirk. "You never know where you've left anything."

Jack hesitated. "Bitz, are you sure? If the crystal isn't where it should be, maybe it's the wrong crystal."

Merle clicked her tongue impatiently. "Jack, there shouldn't be a crystal here at all! Why would anyone put a lump of quartz in a mechanical clock? The Server can look like whatever it wants, remember?"

"Right." Feeling foolish, Jack carefully put The Server down and began to climb into the whirring mechanism, wriggling between shafts and cogs, trying not to touch anything that moved. Merle watched anxiously. Googie climbed up alongside Jack with maddening feline confidence. Bitz paced around below, growling softly. Loaf remained by the clock face, looking down into the square and biting his nails.

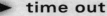

Jack reached the crystal and stopped dead in his tracks.

"Merle." His voice had a faint echo as it floated down to her, barely audible over the workings of the clock. "You remember the exploding pine nut Selenity had?"

"Er . . . yeah?"

"Well, the crystal's sitting in a whole nest of them. Must be a booby trap."

Merle groaned. "Jack, if you drop one of those things, you'll blow this whole place sky-high and bring every FOE on Vered down on our heads!"

"Go ahead," said Jack bitterly, "boost my confidence, why don't you?"

He examined the crystal. It was balanced so that any attempt to move it would dislodge the exploding nuts. "I could try bringing them down one by one."

"There's no time, Jack!" Merle's voice cracked with tension. "Janus and Bitz will be arriving any minute, and when they get here, Bitz says they found the crystal down here, so you have to bring it down. You *have* to."

Cursing, Jack stretched forward to grasp the crystal.

"Easy now," hissed Googie right in Jack's ear, causing him to lose his balance with a startled gasp. "We can't afford any slipups."

Jack glared at the cat. "Will you shut up? I know what I'm doing, okay?" Hardly breathing, he reached for the crystal. "No problem . . . I can do this . . . *there!* Oops!"

He lunged vainly as five of the pine nuts, dislodged from their nest, tumbled in graceful silence toward the floor far below.

Jack gave a despairing cry, "Merle!"

Merle caught one nut, then threw herself headlong to snatch a second one out of the air inches above the ground. She lay gasping, hardly daring to breathe.

At length, she looked up. Loaf was clutching a pine nut in each hand, his trembling fingers clutched around each in a death-grip.

Merle swallowed hard. Well, that was four, but what about the fifth?

Bitz was lying on his back with the fifth nut clasped between all four paws.

Merle stared. "I'm not even going to *ask* how you did that!" She looked up. "Jack, how's about you stop fooling with those things and come down now, whaddaya say?"

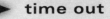

From her perch beside Jack's ear, Googie shook her head in disapproval. "Butterfingers."

"Shut up." Hands trembling, Jack began the perilous climb down.

Several nerve-racking minutes later, he let himself fall the last few feet and leaned wearily against a pillar, gazing at the crystal pulsing in his arms. "What now?"

Merle shrugged. "I'm not sure. We don't know exactly how Janus and Sirius will need us to help."

Help's glowing, hologramatic head appeared. "Whaddaya want?"

Merle frowned at it. "Nobody called you."

"Sure you did, you said, 'Help.'" Help looked around suspiciously. "Hey, this dump looks kinda familiar."

"It's Vered II," said Jack.

Help groaned. "You brought me back here? I am overwhelmed by your consideration! Do you know how many years I spent cooped up in this skid row flophouse?"

"Stop complaining," hissed Jack. "We're here to rescue you."

Help eyed him narrowly. "Hey, primate, you been at the electric banana juice again?"

"Not you *now*, you *then*."

Help shook his head. "Whatever you're paying your psychiatrist, it ain't enough."

Jack held up the crystal so that Help could see it. Help's eyes bulged. "Hey, that's me! Oh, no! Look, guys, just put that thing down and let's get out of here, okay? You're messing with temporal paradoxes that could scramble every reality in the universe, and furthermore, he's a jerk!"

"Who's a jerk?" asked Merle.

"The guy that comes out of there when you say the password 'Friend' and then say 'Help.'" Help broke off suddenly. His hologramatic eyes opened wide in horror. "Now look what you made me do!"

There was a musical *ping* and a hologram appeared above the Crystal Server. A sweet, kindly voice said, "Do you require Help? How may I be of service?"

Jack exchanged glances with Merle. "Uh — we're not sure. We've come here to save you."

The Crystal's Help gave a little squeal of excitement. "To rescue me?" it trilled. "Oh, my

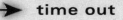

gracious me! After all these years! How exciting!"

Help gave a hollow groan. "What'd I tell you?"

Merle studied the Crystal Server's Help carefully. "He looks like the Help we all know and . . . er . . . know, but different."

"Like Loaf and Lothar." Jack caught Merle's look and bit his tongue. "Sorry."

Merle was right. The Crystal Help looked very much like their Help but shinier and smarter. And a lot more . . . *helpful.*

The hologram beamed at them. "May I be of assistance?"

Jack stared at it. "What?"

"How can I best serve you? It would be my greatest pleasure to assist you in any way."

"See what I mean?" growled Help. "The guy's a creep."

The Crystal Help gave him a kind and vaguely puzzled look. "Have we met?"

Help gazed at his former incarnation with loathing. "Look at it! Yes sir, no sir, three bags full, sir. This is me? I musta been sick."

The Crystal Help beamed. "Gosh! You

mean, you're me in a later incarnation? How amusing." It looked around as if inviting its audience to a rare treat. "This is really remarkably interesting, is it not? To actually meet myself in another disguise. I'm pleased to meet you — or rather, I'm pleased to meet me." The hologram chuckled. "Oh, I'm sorry, I couldn't resist. Just a little joke."

"Yeah, like minuscule," Help seethed. "Somebody *close* it, please!"

Jack gave Bitz a bewildered look. "Our Help used to be like this?"

Bitz looked embarrassed. "Yeah, but then, when we took The Server to Earth and it changed form" — Bitz nodded toward the laptop — "and when I had to carry it in my mouth for months, I guess it must have . . ."

". . . wised up!" snapped Help, giving Bitz a hard stare. "That's what you were going to say?"

Bitz looked Help straight in the eyes. "Something like that," he said flatly.

Loaf, who had been moving his lips as if trying to work something out, suddenly gave Help a narrow-eyed look. "Hey, wait up! We're

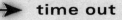

talking to you." He turned to look at the Crystal Help. "I mean, not you *now*, you *back then* . . ." Loaf floundered. "What I mean is, how come you don't remember all this?"

Help gave Bitz another disgusted look. "Aside from *wising up*, another effect of being slobbered on for months on end by Mister Dribbly here is that parts of my memory got corrupted." Help sighed theatrically. "Nobody will ever know what I suffered."

The Crystal Help giggled. "Isn't this *fun*? Now, what shall we do next? Would you like to log on to the Outernet? Or shall we have a stimulating conversation? Or if you prefer, I have a memory full of fascinating games that —"

Jack held up a hand to silence the flow. "Maybe later. Right now we just want you to lie low and keep quiet. Friends are on the way to rescue you. Just go with them, don't make a fuss, and everything will be fine. Okay?"

The Crystal Help gave him an outrageously sly wink. "Anything you say. Mum's the word." It disappeared back into the Crystal Server.

Help rolled its eyes.

Jack turned to Bitz. "We need to leave this exactly where you found it."

Bitz nodded. "Just there."

There was a clatter from the stairwell that had been carved into the dead heart of the tree that led down into the gloom below them.

Bitz turned a stricken face to Jack. "That was me! One of the steps gave way! I'm coming up! I mean, they're coming up! I mean . . ."

Jack gestured urgently to the others, who hurriedly slipped into the shadows beneath a clock face. "Don't panic! Where was The Server? Here?" He set the crystal down.

Bitz shook his head. "Left . . . no, right a bit . . . to you . . . *there*."

Jack grabbed Bitz and dived for cover.

A split second later, a furry face appeared at the top of the stairs and peered cautiously into the room.

Jack watched, hardly daring to breathe, as a Veredian spider-monkey, who could have been the twin of Selenity's pet, Tig, scuttled across the floor and pawed at the crystal, making little cooing sounds.

Jack glanced at Bitz. "That's you?" he whispered.

Bitz nodded. "Nobody notices a spider-monkey on Vered."

Jack felt the dog's body grow tense as another newcomer slipped from the shadows of the stairway and crossed the room. Janus!

The humanoid bent down and picked up the Crystal Server. "Here it is, Sirius," he said softly. "Just where my research said it had to be. The Lost Server of Vered II. The last Server to have escaped The Tyrant's clutches. We have found it in time."

He spoke too soon. There was a rapid fire of shots, which lit up the great workings of the clock like lightning bolts. Orders rang out, and a dozen Bugs charged up the stairs, overwhelming Janus and Sirius before they had time to react or resist. Jack watched in utter despair as The Tyrant's enforcers seized the luckless Friends in grips of steel and marched them away.

Bitz, who had been struck dumb with horror at Janus's arrest, came back to life as the last of the Bugs clattered down the stairway with their captives. The dog wriggled in Jack's grip, growling and snarling in an ecstasy of fury. "Lemme go!" he howled. "I'll bite them on the leg! I'll tear 'em to pieces! I'll widdle in their boots! Lemme at 'em!"

"Calm down!" Jack clung to the wiggling canine. "There's nothing you can do!"

"Yes, there is! I'm gonna chew their big Bug butts!"

"Bite me no butts!" Googie shook her head wearily. "This time line is already screwed up now! Nothing you can do is going to make it right."

"Googie's right, Bitz." Merle stroked the dog's ears soothingly. "We'd all like to help you and Janus, but there's nothing we can do."

Bitz bared his teeth. "You're just making excuses. What's the matter? You all turned chicken?"

"Ah, a question for you, Loaf," said Merle nastily. "Say one cluck for yes, two clucks for no." Loaf glared at her.

"That's enough," said Jack firmly. The bickering stopped. Merle and the others turned to face him. "The whole point of coming here was to get back to our original time line," he

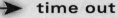

continued. "Right? The one we left to take The Server back to Selenity's time." Bitz gave a grudging nod.

"But we've just seen you and Janus captured," Jack went on. "And The Tyrant is going to get The Server. We know that leads to the time line where Earth gets invaded by The Tyrant. But if we try to rescue you now, that wouldn't take us back to the *right* time line even if we succeeded . . ."

"Which we wouldn't," put in Loaf.

" . . . because that's not the way it happened. You weren't captured. Whatever we do here now will lead to a different time line."

Bitz's tail drooped. "Might be a better one," he muttered defiantly.

"Or it might be worse," said Merle firmly. "The point is, it wouldn't be ours."

"All right, all right." Bitz shrugged angrily.

Jack ruffled Bitz's ears apologetically. "We'd do something if we could."

"I wouldn't," said Loaf. The others glared at him. "Against Bugs? Get real."

"Next in our series, *Profiles in Courage*," said Merle to nobody in particular. *"Loaf: The Man with No Shame."*

Bitz's tail drooped between his legs. "So what *do* we do?"

"Go back," said Jack.

Bitz's ears pricked up. "Back?"

Merle nodded grimly. She bent down and picked up two of the mango-shaped pine nuts from the floor.

Jack nodded. "Back in time again. Once you and Janus have been captured by the FOEs, there's nothing we can do. But there's no reason we shouldn't try to stop the FOEs from capturing you in the first place." He grinned. "Is there?"

CHAPTER EIGHT

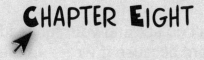

They rematerialized behind a fallen branch in Green Square, on the opposite side from the clock.

Jack's eyes traveled up the dead trunk. "We're just about to arrive up there." He pointed to the nearest face of the clock. "And a few minutes after that, Janus and Bitz will try to take The Server."

Loaf stuck his head around the branch and stared. Jack reached out and hauled him back.

"Keep your head down!" he hissed. "Do you want us to see you?"

Loaf's face was a study in bewilderment. "What?"

"When we were looking out from the clock," Merle whispered, "did you see yourself over here?" Dumbly, Loaf shook his head.

"Then don't go sticking your fat head where it can be seen, because if we — up there — see us — down here, that could send us off into *another* different time line." She gave Loaf a very unfriendly look. "Again."

"You mean we're down here, and we're up there in the clock, as well?" Loaf closed his eyes and groaned. "I can't keep up with all these time lines!"

"Just stay out of sight." Jack gazed around at his companions. "Our job now is to keep the Bugs occupied and divert their attention while Janus and Bitz snatch The Server. Whatever it takes. Do we all know what to do?" He was answered by nods from Merle, Googie, and Bitz, and a shrug from Loaf. "Then let's do it."

A few minutes later, the FOEs team sent to secure the Veredian Server was stopped in its tracks as it crossed the dilapidated and deserted Green Square. An eerie, high-pitched yodel echoed through the trees.

"Aaaaaaa, ah*ahah*aaaaaa, ah*ahah*aaaaaa!"

They looked up. Their jaws dropped.

"Is it a bird?" asked one Bug.

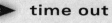

"Is it a plane?" asked another.

A third, who had a better view, said, "No. It appears to be an overweight humanoid swinging on a vine."

Loaf swung back into view, high above. "Ooooooo, oh*oh*oh*oooooo*, oh*oh*oh . . . oh, *noooooooo . . .*"

The disease-weakened vine snapped. Loaf tumbled from branch to branch. He clung to twigs. Twigs clung to him. The Bugs watched his descent with mild interest until he bounced off the last branch and sprawled, winded and covered in bark stains and lichen, at their feet. Then they advanced, weapons raised.

"Hey! Over here, ya big palookas!"

The startled Bugs turned and began to dance a slow, lumbering dance as Bitz and Googie charged into their midst. The dog snapping at their ankles and the cat clawing at their eyes couldn't really do the armored creatures any damage, but they acted as if they could. One or two of the more trigger-happy Bugs started firing at the chameleoids, but succeeded only in hitting their comrades whose outraged roars added to the chaos.

In the confusion, Loaf managed to get his breath back and made a panic-stricken crawl for freedom. Above his head, misaimed weapons barked and hammered. Energy beams surged past his ears as Loaf, squeaking with terror, picked himself up and ran. As Bitz and Googie disengaged, the Bugs turned their attention on the retreating Loaf and took aim.

"Peek-a-boo!" Across the square, Merle stepped out from behind the branch and waved. As the Bugs swiveled toward her, she lobbed something the size and shape of a mango into their midst and dived for cover. Instinctively, the Bugs leaped away from the bouncing object and hurled themselves to the ground.

Loaf had reached cover by the time the Bugs realized that the thing that had been thrown at them wasn't going to explode. Merle watched in dismay as they slowly clambered to their feet. She turned to Jack. "It didn't go off," she said unhappily.

One of the Bugs reached down gingerly, picked up the pine nut that Merle had thrown, and snorted in disgust.

"This is not a grenade," it said in its surprisingly cultured voice. "This is merely a seedpod from one of the trees. It is completely harmless." With a snarl of disgust, it hurled the nut savagely to the ground at its feet.

Merle dived for cover. From the shelter of the fallen branch, she, Jack, and Loaf watched the resulting explosion lift the Bugs off their feet and hurl them clear across the square. They ducked as one of The Tyrant's enforcers, a look of annoyance and astonishment on its face, flew over their heads with a whooshing noise, and fell, crashing through the lower branches of the forest far below.

Jack eyed the blast damage in the center of the square and the stunned Bugs, some of which were now wedged in the forks of trees, or had been blown through the windows of buildings. "As seeds go, those things make pretty good offensive weapons."

Bitz and Googie skidded through the gap underneath the branch. Bitz stood panting, his tongue lolling from the side of his mouth. Googie began to lick her fur. "Can we t-mail out of here now?" demanded the cat.

Jack took another look at the square. One or two Bugs were starting to stand up. He shook his head. "Not yet. We can't be sure we gave Janus and Bitz enough time to grab The Server and get away. We have to keep the Bugs following us." He stood up and waved. "Hey, Buggy-boys! This way!"

The fallen branch began to disintegrate under a hail of fire from the Bugs' weapons.

"I think you got their attention!" yelled Merle.

"I think they're recovering," replied Jack.

Loaf was already crawling for more substantial cover. "I think it's time we were someplace else!"

A few minutes later, the companions were racing along swaying walkways. These weren't the gleaming, shimmering, suspended trails they remembered from their previous visit. Vered City's walkways were now dilapidated, broken, and pitted. The humans slid on piles of slushy leaf mold. Bitz fell behind as he struggled to climb over fallen branches. Googie sped along in the lead, surefooted as ever, sidestepping holes and springing across gaps through which the smoke from the forest floor rose in greasy swirls.

So it was Googie, rounding a corner at top speed, who streaked straight into a hairy, eight-legged being who had been running in the opposite direction. The result was a hissing, snarling, and chirping confusion of limbs and fur that rolled several feet before coming to a stop.

The Veredian spider-monkey Googie had collided with untangled itself and backed off, scolding furiously.

"Sirius!" Googie gave a yowl of frustration. "Did you have to choose *this* way to escape? Can't you do anything right?"

The spider-monkey's fur stood on end. It chirped threateningly. "Who are you? What are you doing here? Are you spying on us?"

"Oh, for pity's sake, lighten up!" the cat said wearily. "I'm on your side."

Sirius gave a hysterical shriek of monkey laughter. "Pull the other seven, FOE." It waved its legs insultingly. "If you're planning on running to tell The Tyrant you've seen us, forget it. You'll have to go through me first."

Googie glared at the eight-legged creature

with narrowed eyes. "Don't think it wouldn't be a pleasure to tear you limb from limb from limb from limb. Good grief, you weren't this stupid even when you were a dog."

Jack and the others skidded to a halt behind Googie. Sirius bared his teeth in a snarl and hastily backed away. More strangers! Who were these people? Certainly no one he'd ever met before!

Jack stared at the spider-monkey. "Googie, I hope that isn't who I think it is."

Running footsteps echoed from farther down the walkway. The mist coiled. A figure burst through a cloud of vapor and, finding the way blocked, came to an abrupt stop.

Jack found himself staring at a humanoid with a determined face, a bald head, and the eyes of a cat. "Janus!"

Janus clutched the Veredian Server tightly and dropped into a fighting crouch. "Sirius, what's going on?"

Bitz gave a whine. "See, Janus, what happened was . . ."

Googie hissed. "He's not talking to you, dog-breath."

The spider-monkey skittered back to stand

beside Janus, whose eyes hadn't flickered away from the companions. "Who are you?"

Jack gave Merle a helpless glance. "Now what do we do?"

Merle shrugged. "Another fine mess," she muttered. She opened the case of the laptop. "Help!"

"Yeah, what?" Help took in his surroundings, his eyes bulging when he saw the crystal form of his previous self. "Oh, for cryin' out loud, ol' fancy-pants is back!"

Simultaneously, the Veredian Server's Help had materialized above its crystal. "We meet again," it said cheerfully. "How is our escape going?" It looked around, taking in Janus's look of complete bafflement. "Oh, dear."

"You said it, dreamboat." Help gave a joyless cackle. "We got us a situation here." The angry hologram glared at Jack. "You were home free, and you blew it!"

"I know!" groaned Jack. "Janus and Bitz — I mean, Sirius — have seen us, so when we meet up on Earth they'll remember us, but they didn't, so in our reality this never happened, which means that our time line is all fouled up *again*!"

Janus relaxed slightly but continued to look baffled. "I didn't understand a word of that."

"Neither did I!" Sirius waved his eight legs in bewilderment. "Who is Bitz?"

"I am," said Bitz. "I mean, you are. I mean, you will be. I mean, I was you, and you're going to be me . . ."

Jack groaned. "Don't make this any more confusing than it is already."

The Crystal Help cleared its throat helpfully. "Actually, it's not as complex as it might appear. What we have here is a fairly simple multidimensional temporal paradox . . ."

"Shut up!" bellowed Jack.

"Well, really!" The Crystal Help sniffed disgustedly and disappeared back into its Server.

Jack turned to Janus. "We're from the future. You're going to meet us and send us to help you get The Server and save you from the Bugs. We did that but we weren't supposed to meet you, and . . ." He threw his arms in the air. "And I don't have a clue what to do next! Help?"

The Crystal Help's head appeared again.

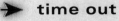

"Yes?" it said in a remote, unfriendly voice. "Was there something you needed?"

"I wasn't talking to you!"

"Manners cost nothing, you know." The head disappeared again.

"Touchy," drawled Help, "isn't he? Well, if you want my advice, you ain't gonna get back to your Earth on this time line. The only thing you can do is loop back in time again, and stop this meeting from happening."

"Yeah? And how are we supposed to do that?" demanded Loaf.

Help gave him a leer. "I'm sure a giant intellect like yours will find a way."

Jack ran his fingers through his hair. "Okay. Do it." He gave Janus an apologetic look. "Sorry, there isn't time for any more explanations. I — er — hope you get away from here. We have to go save our Galaxy now, which is a different galaxy from yours, because it's on a different time line, but good luck with saving your Galaxy, anyway — that is, if it continues to exist after we've gone."

"Coordinates set," announced Help.

With some relief, Jack nodded to Merle,

who pressed the SEND key. He raised a hand in farewell. "Bye."

Janus and Sirius shielded their eyes as a sudden flash of blue-white light enveloped Jack and his companions, and they winked out of existence.

"Whoa!" Loaf pushed himself back against the sloping roof. His breathing came in ragged gasps.

Jack stared down through hundreds of feet of space at the wide, desolate, and above all, hard surface of Green Square, and gulped.

Merle had her eyes shut. "Jack, I don't think this is such a good idea!"

"Ditto," said Bitz faintly.

"What is the matter with you?" Googie was sitting on the ledge that surrounded the decorated roof above the four faces of the Great Clock, calmly washing herself, as if the sheer drop beneath her didn't exist. "You're perfectly safe."

"Googie," wailed Merle, "we're on top of the clock, on a sloping roof with no handholds and nothing but a foot-wide ledge between us

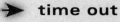

and a long fall to sudden death! In what way would you classify this as 'safe'?"

Googie glanced down casually. "Well, it doesn't bother me."

Merle gave her a savage glare. "Good for you. Aaaaaah!"

Jack shot her a startled glance. "What happened?"

"I looked down."

Loaf, spread-eagled with his back against the roof, said, "Just to make sure I've got a handle on what's happening here: We're out here on the roof . . ."

"Right." Jack nodded carefully.

"And at the same time, we're also inside the clock . . ."

"Yup."

". . . and, I just want to be clear on this, we're also down there in the square."

"You got it."

"Oh, good. For a moment there, I thought this situation was getting complicated."

With extreme caution, Jack inched away from the roof until he could almost see the whole square. "The Bugs are just coming into

view now. We must be over there . . ." He
pointed and instantly lay back down as the
movement threatened to tip him over.

"Aaaaaaa, ahahahaaaaaa, ahahahaaaaaa!"
The cry echoed from below. Jack caught a
glimpse of an unlikely-looking Tarzan swinging from a vine.

"There you go, Loaf." Jack turned his attention to the roof. There was a small round
window, perhaps a skylight, a little distance
away. "Merle, can you get to the window and
see what's going on inside the clock?"

Merle shook her head vehemently. "I'm not
moving!"

Jack muttered something under his breath.
"Okay, stay where you are. I'll have to get past
you." Scooting along with his back against the
roof, Jack inched to his left. When he reached
Merle, he turned over and found himself flattened against her.

Merle opened her eyes to find herself nose-
to-nose with Jack. "What are you doing?"

"I have to get to the window."

"If you make me fall to my death, I'll never
speak to you again!"

Jack reached the window and peered down into the workings of the clock, just in time to see himself lift the Crystal Server and drop the pine nuts. He gave a whistle of appreciation. "Nice catches! Especially Bitz."

Bitz was staring at the drop in front of him with an expression of frozen terror. "It was nothing. Thank you. Don't mention it."

From the square below came the sound of shots as Bitz and Googie attacked the Bugs.

Jack continued to stare through the window. "I'm putting the crystal down now . . . we're all hiding . . . here comes Bitz — I mean, Sirius — and Janus . . . they have The Server . . . they're turning to go . . ."

An explosion echoed around the square. The Bugs had detonated the pine nut.

When his ears had stopped ringing, Jack scrambled to the corner of the clock tower. Far below, he saw Janus, carrying the Crystal Server, and his spider-monkey companion step out from a doorway in the side of the tower facing away from the square. They ran toward a nearby walkway.

Jack groaned. "If they keep on going that

way, they'll meet us! We've got to head them off." He turned his head. "Merle! Throw me the pine nut!"

Merle turned her head and stared at him. "Throw it? Are you crazy? Anyway, I'll fall!"

"No, you won't! And I'll catch the nut." Jack beckoned urgently. "You have to do this! It's our only chance of stopping them."

Cautiously, Merle took the last remaining pine nut from her pocket, steadied herself, and lobbed it to Jack, who had to lean out to catch it.

"Whooooooaaaaa!"

Merle squeaked in horror. "What happened? Did you fall?"

Jack lay back against the roof, breathing hard. "Can't you see for yourself?"

"I've got my eyes shut!"

With a muttered prayer, Jack measured the distance to the walkway far below where Janus and Sirius were making their escape and hurled the deadly seedpod with all his might. The motion sent him tumbling forward.

A hand caught him by the elbow and dragged him back from the brink. Jack turned his head. "Thanks, Merle."

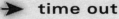

He looked down just in time to see the walkway in front of Janus and Sirius erupt in a ball of flame. The Friends skidded to a halt, hesitated, and turned.

Jack remembered to breathe again. "They're coming back . . . they must think the FOEs are firing at them . . . now they're heading off down another walkway. We did it!"

"Hooray," said Merle faintly. "Can we go now?"

Jack felt the tension draining from his body. Muscles flinched as they relaxed. "Sure."

"About time!" Loaf brightened up. "Earth, here I come! First thing I'm gonna do is get a king-size Coke, a bucket of fries, and a double cheeseburger like Momma used to make!"

Merle carefully crouched down over the keyboard as she tapped in the coordinates that would take them back to Earth.

"Take us home, li'l lady." Beside himself with relief, Loaf slapped Merle on the back.

The force of the blow made Merle stagger. Teetering on the ledge, with nothing but empty air before her, she dropped The Server.

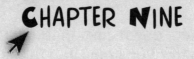

CHAPTER NINE

Five pairs of eyes stared over the ledge at The Server as it hung, half-open, on the minute hand of the Great Clock.

Merle turned to Loaf. Expressions of shock, outrage, and fury swept across her face like ripples on a pond. "Now look what you did!"

Loaf's look of horror was almost comical. "It wasn't my fault! What'd you have to go and drop it for?"

"Drop it? *Drop it?*"

"All right!" Jack's voice was like a whiplash. "We've got to get it back."

Loaf gazed at the vertical drop before them and shuddered. "Count me out!"

There was a confused roar of raised voices from inside the clock room beneath their feet. *Bugs,* Jack thought. They've climbed into the clock. Now they've discovered The Server has gone . . .

Then the Great Clock of Vered II struck the quarter.

Big *bang*, big *bang*
Big *bang*, big *bang*
Big *bang*, big *bang*
Big *bang*, big *bang*!

Swaying, with her hands clamped over her ears and her face screwed up with agony, Merle moaned, "That is LOUD!"

Jack turned to face her. His lips moved. "What?"

Merle shook her head, but the ringing inside it wouldn't go away. "What?"

"We must have arrived here just after it struck the hour." Jack shook his head to clear it. "I'm glad we looped back out of there before those bells struck! The Bugs must have gone deaf! It's bad enough out here."

Merle stuck a finger in her ear and wiggled it about. "What?"

"What?"

Merle felt her hearing begin to return. She

tapped Loaf on the shoulder roughly and pointed at The Server. "Go get it!"

"Huh?" Loaf looked down and shuddered. "You dropped it, you get it."

"I wouldn't have dropped it if you hadn't . . ."

"Shut up, both of you." Jack allowed himself to slide slowly down to the ledge. "I'll get it."

Merle pointed at Loaf. "I don't see why he shouldn't . . ."

"Merle!" Jack was lying on the ledge with one leg already hanging over the drop, his foot feeling for toeholds. "We don't have time to argue about this. The Server is hanging from the minute hand, or whatever the long hand on this clock is called. And it's pointing to a quarter past the hour."

Merle looked down at Jack, shuddered, and quickly looked away again. "So?"

"So, the minute hand is lying horizontal right now because it's a quarter past the hour. But from now on, it's going to move on down to half past. The hand will be pointing vertically down. And somewhere in between . . ."

Merle felt her head swim. "The Server will slide off!"

"Right." Jack swung his body over the edge, hanging from his elbows.

Far below, a stream of Bugs poured out of the tower. With their hands clamped firmly over their ears, they staggered off in pursuit of Janus and Sirius.

Merle watched, terrified, as Jack lowered himself farther. "Jack, be careful! You could fall."

Jack shot her a glance. "Would that matter? I'm just a two-bit nobody, remember?"

"I didn't mean that." Steeling herself, Merle knelt down on the parapet to bring her closer to Jack. "You don't have to do this."

Jack looked from Loaf, leaning petrified against the roof, to Bitz, who had his eyes shut and was whining softly, to Googie, who put her head on one side and gave an interrogative meow. "Who else is going to?" He inched down the clock face to hang by his fingertips. Her heart beating like a tom-tom, Merle knelt on the ledge and peered over to watch.

The clock face was divided by metal girders

like the spokes of a wheel, radiating across its translucent dial from the center to each of the sixteen-hour divisions of the Veredian day. Their surface was pitted with rust, providing just enough cracks and crevices to hang onto. Jack inched his way down the girder in the one o'clock position, hanging on for dear life.

Halfway down, he slipped. Merle put her hand to her mouth. "Jack!"

Feet scrabbling frantically, Jack regained his hold. Merle let out her breath with a gasp. "Hold on tight!" she called.

Below her, Jack hugged the rough girder and fought to control his breathing. "I'll try to keep that in mind!" He inched onward.

After a time, his arms and legs trembling with effort, Jack finally stood on the minute hand beside its hub, where the corroded shaft from the clock mechanism held it and the hour hand in place. The minute hand was already falling. It had dipped about ten degrees below its horizontal position, and he could feel the faint tremor of the clockwork through the soles of his sneakers as the hand moved slowly but steadily down.

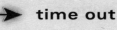

Loaf's voice floated down from the top of the tower. "Has he fallen off yet?"

Merle's hissed reply was inaudible.

Hardly daring to breathe, Jack shuffled along the minute hand. The farther he got from the clock's center, the more the hand shook and swayed under the unaccustomed weight. Cold beads of sweat stung Jack's eyes.

The minute hand had dropped another ten degrees by the time Jack had dragged himself to within touching distance of The Server. With infinite caution, he bent his knees and began to reach down.

The minute hand dipped. Jack swayed and clutched frantically for a hold. He hung upside down from the minute hand, with his hands and legs wrapped around it, like a luckless explorer on his way to the cannibals' pot. His blood felt like ice water. "Oh, help!" he whispered.

There was a flash of silver as a hologramatic head popped into existence over The Server's keyboard — also upside down. "Waddaya wan — whooooaaaaaaa! What am I doing up here? Get me down! Get me down NOW!"

"That's what I'm trying to do!" yelled Jack.

"Listen, you crazy monkey!" screeched Help. "You may think swinging around in the trees is just great, but some of us don't like heights! Am I getting through to you?"

"How can you be scared of heights? You're a computer!"

"A computer with a fully functional self-preservation chip, and right now it's in vertigo overload! I'm gonna fall! Save me! Oh, mercy!" Help gave an earwax-melting electronic scream.

"Will you shut up?" demanded Jack. "I'm trying to reach you."

"Oh, motherboard, I don't wanna die! I don't deserve this, I've tried to live a good virtual life! Somebody save me, I'm too young to be shut down, any second now I'm gonna fall, and it'll be 'Arrivederci, ROM,' Aaaaaaah!"

"I'm nearly there . . ." Jack stretched his trembling fingers to the limit. . . . They brushed The Server's casing. . . .

The hand dipped again. The Server began to slide. Jack lunged for it. . . .

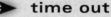

The hologram screamed, "I'm goin'! I'm goin'! Oh, noooooooooooooooo!"

Slipping from Jack's anxiously clutching fingers, The Server slid off the end of the clock hand. With a final shriek of terror from Help, it spiraled down and, as Jack watched in horror, struck the unyielding surface of the square, bounced, and lay still.

Then Jack lost his grip. He slid down the hand and grabbed frantically at the heart-shaped bulge on its end. Weakened by age and Jack's frenzied struggles, the hand jerked violently as it slipped from its cog onto the end of the shaft that held it in place. It hung, trembling, on the brink, swinging dangerously. And Jack hung from it. His hands, damp with sweat from his effort, began to slip.

He looked up. No sign of Merle or Loaf above him. *They were probably lying flat against the roof,* Jack thought angrily, *making sure they were safe while I'm hanging from . . . slipping from . . . this clock hand. . . .*

Jack's fingers reached the end of their strength and let go. He dropped.

He was still filling his lungs with air for a final scream when he felt an arm wrap around his chest. He turned his head. Loaf was leaning out from a jagged hole in the clock face between two of the girders. His face was a mask of terror, but he held on to Jack and didn't let go. Grunting with the effort, Loaf hauled Jack up and through the broken dial, into the safety of the clock room.

Bitz leaped up at Jack, barking frantically. Merle flung her arms around Jack. "You're okay!"

Jack clung onto Merle, trembling from his ordeal. "Where did you two come from? Not that I'm complaining . . ."

Merle stepped away from Jack and stamped her foot at Bitz. "Will you shut up? I can't hear myself think!" She pointed upward. "We came in through the window up there. There's a walkway just below it, so it's easier than it looks. You seemed to be having a few problems, so we thought we'd better come down and give you a hand."

Jack let out his breath in a long sigh. "I sure needed one." He turned to face Loaf. "Thanks."

Loaf looked back to the gap in the clock face and shuddered. "I can't believe I did that!"

Jack gripped Loaf's shoulder. "I owe you one."

Loaf was recovering. The familiar twisted grin reappeared. "Yeah? I may remind you of that someday."

Bitz was still yapping constantly. Jack knelt beside him. "It's great to see you, too." Bitz gave an angry snarl, raced to the head of the stairwell, and looked back expectantly.

Merle, looking puzzled, watched the dog. "I don't think he's telling you he's glad to see you. I think he's worried about . . ."

Jack slapped the side of his head and groaned, "The Server!"

He sprinted for the stairwell. Bitz turned and raced ahead, clearing the rotting wooden steps three at a time. Merle clattered behind him, with Googie at her heels. Loaf brought up the rear, slipping and gasping for breath as they pounded down the spiral staircase cut through the dead heart of the ancient tree.

Very shortly, they emerged from the tree trunk and panted to a halt around The Server, which lay open, its screen and keyboard lying facedown on the concrete. Jack reached out and picked it up.

Help lay squashed against the screen. Before their amazed eyes, the hologram popped into 3-D form like a cartoon character recovering from an encounter with a steamroller. Help instantly conjured itself a head bandage and rolled its eyes while a flock of tiny virtual birds flew in circles around its head making *cheep-cheep* noises.

"My head," moaned the hologram. "What hit me? Did somebody get his number? Call me an ambulance! No! Call my lawyer!"

Merle gasped in astonishment and relief. "I don't believe it! You're okay!"

Help's pathetically confused persona vanished instantly. "Okay? I'm okay? You drop me hundreds of feet onto solid concrete — what have you got against me, for cryin' out loud? — And then you tell me I'm okay? Well, no thanks to you if I am! I may be built to withstand severe shocks, but a fall like that could invalidate my warranty. I hope you realize that." Help gave a disdainful sniff. "Who are your friends?"

"Friends? What friends?" Puzzled, Jack glanced behind him. Then, with a cry of shock,

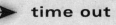

spun around. One by one, his companions did likewise and stared at the black-clad Veredians who had surrounded them while their attention had been on The Server.

Their leader stepped forward. A badge on his uniform showed two white clenched fists. His beak was tilted disdainfully, his face set in an arrogant sneer.

"You are breaking the curfew." His voice was harsh with contempt.

Jack returned his hard stare. "Has the curfew started? We didn't know."

"It is curfew all the time in Vered City." The leader of the Hard Fists gang cast a disgusted look over the companions. "Strangers!" he snapped, his beak clicking like bad-fitting dentures. "Aliens! Degenerates! Subversives! How dare you pollute our Veredian soil with your loathsome presence!"

Merle had had a bad day. Pushing Jack aside, she confronted the Veredian. "In the first place, we're not on your soil, we're on your concrete. In the second place, it looks like you already did all the polluting this place can handle before we got here. And in the third place, we've met your kind before, and they were a bunch of lightweight creeps, and so are you. So back off."

The Veredian blinked. Then it drew back both its right arms and slapped Merle across the face, one stinging blow following the other so fast that the astonished girl had no time to duck. Merle slowly raised her hand to her cheek. Her face twisted. "Why you . . ."

She leaped at the Hard Fist leader — or tried to. Jack and Loaf, one on each side, grabbed her before she'd gone half a step, and held her back despite her struggles.

"Let me go!" snarled Merle, beside herself with fury. "I'll rip his face off."

"Calm down!" Jack's voice was sharp. "There are more of them than there are of us, and they're armed and we're not."

"They're just thugs," snarled Merle.

"Yes," agreed Jack, "but organized thugs. Disciplined thugs. They're not just bullies like Tyro Rhomer."

"Tyro Rhomer?" The Veredian's eyes widened with astonishment. "You dare to utter the name of one of the heroes of the Hard Fist Revolution?"

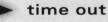

Jack glared at him. "Hero? I'm talking about Tyro Rhomer, the coward who tried to beat up a friend of ours and ran like a scared rabbit when we stopped him."

The Veredian's eyes glittered. Blood vessels stood out beneath his skin and his voice shook with fury as he snarled, "I was going to arrest you and find out what you are doing here. But I have just lost interest in anything further you might have to say." He reached for a holster on his belt and drew a blaster. "Shoot them where they stand."

The gang reached for their weapons.

A sudden gust of wind rattled through the few remaining leaves of the forest canopy. Jack looked up.

High above them, the minute hand of the Great Clock of Vered II had not moved. Dislodged from the cog that should have swept it around the face, it still hung at half past the hour. The wind struck it.

It swayed. For a second, it remained, trembling on the very outer lip of the shaft that had held it for so long. Then it fell.

The hand plummeted down like an arrow. It made a whistling sound as it fell. The leader of the Hard Fists looked up, opened his mouth, screamed, and flung up all four arms in futile defense. There was a terrible *thud!*

Merle gave a gasp and turned away, shuddering.

Jack stared in horror at the remains of the gang leader. "Like a butterfly pinned to a board!"

Loaf said in a very flat voice, "I guess his time just ran out."

The companions turned to face the remaining thugs.

The other Hard Fists looked at their fallen leader. They looked at Bitz, fur standing on end, teeth bared. They looked at Googie, lips drawn back in a snarl, tail bushy. They looked at Loaf and Merle. They looked at Jack.

They dropped their weapons and ran.

Jack sighed. His shoulders slumped. He passed The Server to Merle.

"I guess that puts us back on our own time line. Set the coordinates for Earth," he said wearily. "Take us home."

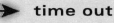

Stonehenge, Planet Earth, Sol System
One year ago

As Jack was speaking, a hundred light-years away, a small dog lay in the shadow of one of the great stones of Stonehenge.

It watched as a patrol of Bugs trooped into the center of the circle, which flared blue-white, t-mailing them to a distant sector of the Galaxy in their fruitless search for The Server, which lay on the ground between Sirius's front paws.

The Friends agent watched them go. He gave a scornful sniff. In his own language, he muttered, "Suckers!"

With some difficulty, he picked up The Server in his mouth and trotted resolutely off into the night.

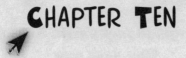

CHAPTER TEN

N-Space

They were inside a log cabin. A fire burned in a huge stone fireplace. Smells of home-cooked food wafted through the air.

It wasn't real. Jack glanced through the window to see flows of particles cascading down in a never-ending stream. Storms of pure energy fizzled and crackled. Colors assaulted the eye in a multidimensional spectral display.

"N-space!" moaned Loaf. "Not again."

"Whose memory is it this time?" asked Jack. He looked toward Merle and had his answer.

She was staring silently at the picture frames that lined the walls.

"It's our vacation home," murmured Merle, "near the lake."

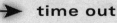

The smells of cooking were having an effect on Loaf. He moaned. "Man, am I hungry. All this traveling and the only thing I've eaten is alien junk. Beetles and leaves are not enough for a growing boy."

"I'm afraid it is purely imaginary." Janus stepped forward to greet the travelers. Bitz gave a welcome yelp.

"Tell my stomach that," said Loaf. "I need some real food now. Burgers, doughnuts . . ."

"Why here?" cut in Merle.

Janus gave a smile. "To thank you for what you have done."

Merle walked over to the fireplace and looked at the photographs on the mantel. Pictures of her family, her mom, her dad, herself as a baby. More memories flooded back and she smiled.

The others looked on, not knowing what to think or do.

Eventually, Merle breathed deeply and turned to face the others. "Mom's dead. She's not coming back. I know that."

There was a brief silence before Googie padded over to Merle and arched protectively against her leg. Merle bent down and stroked her cat. "Thanks, Googie," she said. She looked up at Janus. "That's why you created this room and brought us back to N-space, wasn't it? Closure."

"Partly," answered Janus. "And also to congratulate you on a successful mission and inform you what must happen now."

"Go back to Vered and rescue Lothar?" suggested Merle, hoping against hope.

Janus's face was grave. He shook his head slowly. "I'm afraid not."

"But we've done everything you asked," protested Merle. "And more . . ."

Janus looked deep into Merle's eyes. "When does a Friend's duty end? On the point of death? Or . . ." — He gestured at the surroundings — ". . . even beyond that?"

"He was *my* friend," argued Merle. "Where does my duty end to him?"

Janus was silent.

"Merle . . ." began Jack.

"Jack, he's marooned," protested Merle. "No family, no friends, no past . . ."

"But he has a future," insisted Janus. "One that you have helped to save and shape through your selfless actions."

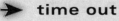

"But . . ." Merle's protest ebbed away as acceptance of the situation took hold of her.

"All beings have their roles to play," continued Janus. "Perhaps one day, you will meet with Lothar again."

Jack stared into Janus's yellow eyes. "You know, don't you?"

"There are still many paths to follow, many possibilities that could come about. Nothing is certain."

"So what happens now?" asked Jack.

"The foundations for your future have been laid," answered Janus. "Your time line is rescued. The Outernet will grow, and, with it, hope for every being in the Galaxy."

"Well, yea for that!" said Loaf sarcastically. "And who messed it all up in the first place?" He pointed an accusing finger at Bitz and then Janus. "Arriving on Earth with The Server. Did we ask to be involved in all of this? I don't think so."

Janus's voice became harsh. "In many stories that are told throughout the Galaxy, the most reluctant participant may become a hero. Or a villain," he added.

"Where does this story end?" asked Jack.

"Do stories ever have a final ending?" Janus gave a faint smile. "Humans! Always wanting the end before they have completed the journey. Do not worry, Jack, in time you will have your ending. But it may not be the one you wish for."

Loaf yawned. "Well, I want to end up back home, and the sooner the better."

"And so you will. You are all to return to Earth and continue your protection of The Server."

"And what else?" asked Loaf. "What's the new mission that we have to accept?"

"Events will take their course," answered Janus. "You will respond to them."

Googie gave a disgusted meow. "You're saying that we have to sit around until something happens!"

Loaf shook his head. "Sit around? Oh, well, I suppose we can play around with a little time travel."

Janus shook his head. "Once you have traveled back to your own time line on Earth, The Server's time travel capability will be disabled."

"Why?" demanded Merle.

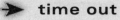

Janus sighed. "With time travel, there are far too many opportunities for time lines to distort and change and for paradoxes to occur. As you have already experienced," he added.

"You are soooo right," said Googie.

"Your original task is not yet over," continued Janus. "You still have to deliver The Server to The Weaver. The tasks you have accomplished so far are merely stepping-stones to the final destination."

"Do you know who The Weaver is?" asked Bitz. "And if you do, where do we find him?"

"All will soon be revealed," replied Janus.

"You haven't answered the question," said Merle. "If Selenity wasn't The Weaver then do you know who The Weaver really is?"

Janus shook his head. "I cannot tell you."

"Why not?!" wailed Merle. "You never tell us anything! When you sent us back in time to meet Selenity on Vered, you knew we had to download The Server's knowledge into his computer — but you didn't even tell us that!"

"If I had," said Janus, "you would not have argued with Jack. You would not have gone to the alternative Earth."

"And that's something I had to do? For the future of the Outernet?"

"Yes."

"Why?"

Janus shook his head. "I can't tell you. You see? Every question leads to more questions. The answers would alter the way you behave, react, and put the future — the Galaxy's future — in danger.

"If you know the identity of The Weaver, your knowledge would interfere with the time line you are following. All is still possible. All may change. In the meantime, it is necessary to keep The Server safe. You must trust me."

Bitz nodded. "That goes without saying."

Janus smiled and turned to the others.

After a few seconds, Jack nodded and Loaf shrugged his shoulders. Googie arched her back. "If it means I can finally go home without worrying about The Tyrant, I'm all for it."

"And you?" asked Janus.

Everyone stared at Merle. She sighed. "Yes. If I have to."

"And now return to Earth. You will soon be contacted."

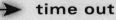

"Contacted? By who?" asked Jack.

"That is all I can tell you. It is time for you to return home." Janus motioned toward The Server. A stream of energy flared from his fingertips and enveloped the black box. "The coordinates are set." He made the secret sign of Friendship. "Go well."

Loaf gave a sarcastic little wave. "Well, nice seeing you again, keep in touch. Don't be a stranger."

His words were drowned out as the companions were once again enclosed in a whirlpool of blue-and-white light and sent on their way.

U.S. Air Force Base, Lower Slaughter, near Cambridge, England Present day

"It looks like your house, or are we in some sort of parallel paradox thingy again?" asked Loaf.

All five Friends looked around, taking in their latest surroundings. It was dark outside. Merle switched on a light and gave a relieved nod. "Looks like it, but after what's been happening, I couldn't give you a hundred percent affirmative," she said. "Let's ask Help."

The hologram shot out from The Server. "Hey! Who's been rifling through my files and dumping my programs without my permission?" it demanded.

"Like what?" asked Loaf.

"Like the time travel teleportation software, monkey-brain. It's gone. It is no more. It is a deleted application."

"Janus got rid of it," Jack explained. "To make sure there's no more historical changes."

"What a spoilsport!" moaned Help. "Just when I was getting the hang of it."

"Well, it's gone," said Jack. "So stop moaning and tell us where we are."

"Sheesh," complained Help. "What am I, a road map?"

"Just tell us," demanded Googie, "or there'll be more deletions . . ." The threat was left hanging in the air.

Help gave a whistle. "Whoa, don't be such a sourpuss. You're home. Well, obviously not you two shape-shifters. I mean, the primates are home. It's Earth. Like you wanted. Right

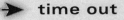

place, right time. Everything back to normal."
The hologram shot Loaf a look. "Or as normal
as some of you are ever gonna get."

"And how long have we been gone?"
asked Jack.

"And now I'm a diary!" snapped Help. He
caught Googie's stare. "Ten days since you
were last here."

"Seems longer," mused Jack.

"It *has* been longer!" said Loaf. "We've
been shooting across the Galaxy. Bouncing
around planets, traveling on spaceships. I
think we're all due for a big dose of jet lag.
And I'm due for a big dose of double cow in a
bun with extra fries."

He was stopped by a cry from Jack, who
had picked up a newspaper lying on the table.
"We're in trouble."

Loaf snorted. "You don't say!" he exclaimed. "We've been shot at, attacked by
aliens, boldly been to more dangerous places
than the Starship *Enterprise* and the *Millen-
nium Falcon* put together, and you say we're
in trouble!" Loaf began to applaud. "Congrat-
ulations, Jack Armstrong. You receive an
A-double-plus for stating the obvious."

"Look at this." Jack tossed the newspaper toward Loaf. He caught it and read the front-page headline:

FEARS GROW FOR MISSING TEENAGERS

"Let me see!" Merle snatched the paper and scanned the article. "It's about us! . . . *Police alerted . . . nationwide hunt . . .* ("Should have tried Galaxy-wide," interjected Bitz.) *No idea where they have gone . . . Strange happenings at air base . . . parents worried sick . . .*"

Loaf gave a bitter laugh. "Not mine."

"Mine will be," said Jack.

"My dad, too," added Merle.

"Sentimentalists," meowed Googie. "I haven't seen my parents since I was a larva."

"This is different," responded Merle. "How are we going to tell everyone what's been going on? They won't believe us."

"It hardly matters. It's the Galaxy that matters," Bitz pointed out.

Merle waved the paper. "And what do we do about this?"

The room exploded with opinions and arguments.

"Ignore it. We sit here and wait to be contacted," insisted Bitz.

"We have to tell someone we're back," countered Merle.

"We do what Janus said. We wait."

"For how long?" pushed Merle.

"For as long as it takes."

"Do we have time for that?"

As the five Friends argued over the best course of action, they were unaware that time was closing in on them. Outside, crouched in the shadows below Merle's window and listening to the raised voices, a strange-looking figure smiled to itself. The humans had returned! The figure flicked open a wrist communicator, punched at the buttons with long green fingers, and began to whisper into it.

The message was beamed up through the night sky and continued its journey across the vast reaches of the Galaxy. Within the blink of a stellar explosion, it reached its intended recipient.

The hooded figure listened to the message. A brief smile flickered across its features.

The communication ended.

Its recipient gave a low chuckle and hissed in a voice that was as cold as the depths of space, "So they're back. And now it's my turn." Its thin lips curled in a mirthless smile. "All in good time . . ."

**There's something out there . . .
And it's the next**

#5 the hunt

The Pyramids, near Cairo, Egypt

Merle's phone rang as she ran. She grabbed it from her jacket pocket and pressed the TALK key.

"Hi, Dad . . . look, this isn't a great time right now . . ." Merle ran with both hands clasped to her head, one holding her phone, the other pressed against her ear so she could hear her father's distant voice against the infuriated roars of the pursuing creature. "Yeah, they've caught up with us . . . we're being chased by the Sphinx . . . the Sphinx . . . *S-p-h-i-n-x* . . . you know, two hundred feet long, weighs about a million pounds, woman's head, lion's body . . . yeah! Hang on, I'm gonna lose you, we're going into a pyramid . . . *py-ra-mid* . . . oh, nuts!"

She flipped the phone closed and dodged

to the side as the Sphinx pounced. In spite of its catlike agility, the android guardian was too massive to turn quickly. By the time it had changed direction, Merle was panting up the steps to the narrow entrance to the Great Pyramid where she joined the others in a narrow entryway. The Sphinx's yowls of frustration from outside dislodged fragments of stone from the ceiling. Merle held out the phone. "I said bringing this thing was a bad idea . . . now what?"

Jack shook a barred steel door. "It's locked. We can't get in."

"Am . . . ateurs." Though Loaf was winded by the long run through soft sand, he was excited about his sudden position of importance. "Step . . . aside." He took a piece of bent wire from his bag and set to work on the lock. Seconds later, he was rewarded with a sharp click, and the door swung open.

Loaf stepped aside. "Ta-daaa!"

From outside came a ringing command. The Sphinx hissed. Jack peered outside and grabbed Loaf's arm with renewed urgency. "Come on!"

"What's your hurry?" protested Loaf. "That

thing is mean, but it's way too big to get in here."

"It's got backup," Jack reported. "The woman who nearly caught us in Ops, and some guy with a dog's head, and they *aren't*."

"Aren't what?"

"Too big to get in here. Come *on*!"

The first corridor led downward. After stumbling in the dark for a couple seconds, Jack flipped open The Server. "Help!"

The hologram appeared. "Hey, primate! Where are we now? It's as dark as a tomb in here!"

"Well spotted," said Jack tightly. "How about some light?"

"For you, anything," sneered Help. But it closed its eyes and blew out its hologramatic cheeks as if concentrating, and its head began to glow with the radiance of a low-powered lightbulb.

The companions found themselves standing at the junction of two corridors. One continued to descend, the other climbed away into darkness.

"Down," said Jack, "or up?"

"Up," grunted Loaf, repressing a shudder.

Jack shrugged and started to climb. At first, the passageway was narrow and very low, but after they passed another junction, the passage opened up and the roof soared to more than four times human height. Spurred on by noises from the passage below, the companions clambered up the forty-five-degree slope with all the speed they could muster.

At length, they stopped, gasping, in a chamber large enough to hold a double-decker bus. A huge lidless sarcophagus lay to one side of the chamber. Loaf drew back from it. Merle hoisted herself up and peered inside.

"Relax," she told Loaf cheerfully. "Nobody home."

Jack stared around at the featureless walls. "There's nothing here!"

"Hey, Help!" snapped Bitz. "You want to bring on the ultra-red again?"

"Work, work, work!" grumbled Help, but the glow from his hologramatic head dimmed, and his features turned the red-purple color the companions had first seen at Stonehenge.

Almost immediately, glowing patterns began to emerge on the walls of the chamber.

"Hieroglyphics," said Merle. She picked up

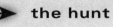

Googie, who for once made no protest. The cat wanted to see the picture-writing close-up.

"C'mon, Help!" snapped Bitz. "Which one do we press?"

"Give me time, willya?" demanded Help. "Now, lemme see — accessing Rosetta Stone files — if the mouth shape is the sound *r* and the owl means 'he', then . . . got it," snapped Help. "Press the bird symbol." Loaf, who was nearest, did so. A section of wall just below the symbol slid back and aside. In the secret compartment revealed behind it lay a golden cross with a loop on the top.

"It's an ankh," said Help curtly, "symbol of eternity. It's the key. Turn it. Three-sixty."

Loaf turned the ankh a full circle. Immediately, a low hum began to resonate through the chamber. The walls began to glow.

"Take it," Help commanded. "We'll need it to activate the other sites." Obediently, Loaf snatched the ankh from its niche.

Jack was breathing hard. "Okay," he said, "how do we get out of here?"

"You don't. Time's up!" The new voice came from the chamber entrance.

Jack turned slowly. The hunter who called

herself Tingkat Bumbung was standing behind him, alongside a human figure with the
head of a dog . . . or a jackal.

Tingkat leveled an energy weapon at the
companions. "Give me The Server . . ."

About the Authors

Steve Barlow and Steve Skidmore

Steve and Steve are both humans of an indeterminate age who have been writing books for young life-forms for more than thirteen Earth years. They live in England with their pets, families, and other aliens. They are presently working on the Zargian version of Outernet but are finding the spelling very difficult.

About the Website

Creative Director: Jason Page
Illustration, design, and programming: Table Top Joe
Additional illustration: Mark Hilton
Script by Steve Barlow, Steve Skidmore, and Jason Page

About You and the Outernet

Once you've logged on to the Outernet, use this space to record your identification.

AGENT ID _____
PASSWORDS _____
_____
_____

OUTERNET™

FROM: The Weaver (address unknown)
TO: New Outernet User

RE: Security Breach

Greetings, unidentified life-form. Mel, a DRAMA official,
has discovered your download and has tracked it to this location.
He has already told a huge FIB agent that you – and possibly
your friends – now know of the existence of the Outernet.
Because the Forces of Evil also may have located
you – we see no alternative but to recruit you.

Proceed directly to the link below to:

• Report to FIB and become a Friends Agent with your own secret identity
• Take part in top secret missions to defeat the Forces of Evil (FOEs)
• Send and receive Outernet mail with other Friends on the Outernet
• Explore alien sites and gather more information on individuals
and their worlds

Good luck, Friend, and remember…Preserve your Link…maintain the Chain.

www.go2outer.net

ONW702

You never know what he'll dig up.

Meet McGrowl—the courageous canine who's bionic to the bone.

When a bizarre vet turns a decidedly average dog into a bionic beastie, the world's furriest, funniest superhero is born!

You Can Find McGrowl Wherever Books Are Sold
www.scholastic.com/kids